Silent Knight

This book is a work of fiction. Any resemblance to actual events or persons, living or dead, is entirely coincidental.

"Silent Knight," by Jody Slyman. ISBN 1-58939-931-5.

Published 2006 by Virtualbookworm.com Publishing Inc., P.O. Box 9949, College Station, TX 77842, US. ©2006, Jody Slyman. All rights reserved. No part of this publication may be reproduced, stored in a retrieval system, or transmitted in any form or by any means, electronic, mechanical, recording or otherwise, without the prior written permission of Jody Slyman.

Manufactured in the United States of America.

This book is dedicated to my cousin, Kayla Chavez. I've had the pleasure of watching you grow into an incredible young woman and our love for each other has held strong, if not grown over the years. Now separated by the miles, we still remain so very close. I love you little cousin.

Silent Knight

by

Jody Slyman

Introduction

DATE - February 14th, 2040
San Francisco, CA

The noon sun starts to break through the gray clouds. The temperature has risen to the low sixties. Pamela Daniels, a now aging grandmother, is in her bedroom getting dressed in a nice black, female suit with a solid white blouse. She is about 5'4" tall and holds a trim build with aging red hair and green eyes.

Pamela hollers out the bedroom door, "Are you kids about ready?!"

Four young voices, two boys and two girls, reply within seconds of each other, "Yes!"

As Pamela finishes getting ready, she grabs a green stress candle and a book of matches from her dresser. She walks out of her bedroom and down stairs into the kitchen. She is there about a minute when a small, five year old girl walks in. The little girl has long blonde hair and blue eyes. The girl is wearing a nice yellow and white flower patterned dress.

The little girl looks at Pamela, "Hi grandma."

Pamela looks down at the little girl, "Hello Piper. Don't you look lovely."

1

About that time, two young boys walk in the kitchen. One is nine and the other is eleven. The nine year old is wearing blue jeans and a blue and white stripped, collared shirt. He has short brown hair and brown eyes. The eleven year old is wearing a pair of black jeans and a solid white collared shirt. He has short brown hair and green eyes.

The nine year old looks at Pamela, "Hi grandma."

Pamela looks over to him, "Well, hello Cody." She looks at the other boy, "And Josh."

Josh smiles, "Hi grandma."

In another minute, a young teenage girl walks into the kitchen. She has shoulder length brown hair and blue eyes. She is wearing tight fitting Calvin Klein jeans and a tight fitting Calvin Klein, long sleeve top.

Pamela looks at the young lady, "Happy birthday Kristen. What are you today, fifteen?"

Kristen smiles, "Yep, and one more year before I get my wheels."

Pamela laughs lightly, "Everybody load up. We have a stop to make before the party."

The five of them exit out the side door of the kitchen, leading out to a covered carport. Sitting there is a forest green, four door, Ford Taurus. Pamela gets in the driver's seat. Kristen gets in the passenger's seat and the other three get in the back. They drive through the suburbs of San Francisco for about twenty minutes. They pass through some nice neighborhoods until they pull up to a cemetery. Pamela pulls into the Parkview Cemetery and drives about a quarter mile in, then stops the car.

Pamela puts the car in park and turns off the engine, "I won't be long."

Kristen unbuckles her seatbelt, "Can I come with you grandma?"

2

Pamela grabs the candle and matches, "Of course dear."

The two of them get out of the car. Kristen walks around the front of the car and over next to Pamela. The two of them start walking towards a tall oak tree. The ground is still damp from the early morning rain and the smell of rain still lingers in the air.

As they walk, Kristen speaks, "Every Valentine's Day you come here and light a candle on the same grave." She pauses, "Is it grandpa's grave?"

Pamela answers, "No dear. It's not grandpa's."

About twenty five yards from the car, they stop by the oak tree and next to the tree is a weather worn, gray marble headstone that lays flat against the ground. It is an extended headstone that contains two names. Though worn, all the words are still readable. Pamela and Kristen look down at the headstone.

Centered at the top of the headstone is carved the words, "Eternal Love". Just below those words, on the left hand side as looking down at the headstone from in front of it is carved the name, "Kristen L. Shobe". Just below the name is carved the words, "Born: Feb 14th, 1973". Just below that date is carved the words, "Died: Sep 28th, 1997".

Just below the words eternal love, on the right hand side as looking down on the headstone from in front of it, is carved the name, "Joseph W. Thompson". Just below that name is carved the words, "Born: Jan 1st, 1973". Just below that date is carved the words, "Died: Feb 14th, 2001". Centered at the bottom of the headstone is a small carved out circle.

Kristen looks at her grandmother, "Joseph Thompson, wasn't he the Silent Knight?"

Pamela nods, "Yes he was." She pauses, "I worked the Silent Knight case when I first became a detective."

Kristen gets a puzzled look, "You never mentioned that before grandma."

Pamela smiles, "Well, it was a long time ago. I'll tell you about it some day."

Kristen looks at the headstone, "So why are we here?"

Pamela bends down and places the candle in the carved out circle at the bottom of the headstone, "I made a promise, on February 14th, 2001."

She lights the candle and stands back up next to Kristen.

Pamela speaks, "Honey, I'm not going to be around forever, so I need to ask you something. It's very important."

Kristen looks at Pamela, "What is it grandma?"

Pamela looks at Kristen, "Promise me, as I did 39 years ago, that when I no longer can, you will come here every year on this day and light a candle as I have." She pauses, "I know it is asking a lot, but I'm asking you because I know I can trust you."

Kristen gets a funny smile, "I don't understand."

Pamela smiles in return, "I too didn't understand at first. This is an eternal flame for an eternal love." She sighs, "All I know is that this flame must never go out. So, please promise me you'll do it."

Kristen shakes her head slightly and looks back at the headstone. Her eyes fix on the date Kristen Shobe was born and then the date Joseph Thompson died. The day he died was the day her grandmother mentioned the promise. She fixes on the words "Eternal Love" and the burning candle and she knows that it must mean something. Her heart beats a little faster when she realizes her first name and middle initial is the same as Kristen Shobe's. She wonders what Kristen Shobe was like.

Finally, Kristen speaks, "Okay grandma." She sighs and smiles, "I promise."

Chapter 1

DATE - January 1st, 1973

Alaska

The snow continues to fall, along with the temperature, and cover the small village just northeast of Hughes, Alaska near Mt George. Jess Thompson, a fairly attractive and well built young man in his mid-twenties, is dressed in animal skins from head to toe. He stands around 5'9" tall and weighs around 170 pounds. He has short brown hair and blue eyes. Jess stands just inside the door of a small hut, watching his wife, Kathy, a beautiful brunette in her late twenties, enter her fourteenth hour of labor. She lays on a blanket of animal skins. She is about 5'4" tall and weighs a trim 120 pounds when she is not pregnant. Kathy has long brown hair and brown eyes. The village doctor, an elderly Native American, continues to talk her through the birth. Jess looks up at the roof of the hut and wonders if moving to Alaska to start a new life was a good idea. He also wonders, boy or girl?

Suddenly, a baby's cry fills the hut. Jess is drawn back into reality and looks over to see the doctor wrapping an animal skin around the baby. The doctor hands the baby to a weakened Kathy. The doctor smiles at Kathy, then gets up and walks over to Jess.

The doctor smiles, "You have a son."

Jess lets out a sigh, "Thanks, for everything."

The doctor nods, "All I can say is that I've never seen a baby make it through a birth like that, in conditions like these." He pauses, "Your son is very unique and very special."

As the doctor opens the door, Jess turns to him, "Thanks again. By the way, I didn't get your name."

The doctor looks back at Jess, "I'm Joseph Takotna, and you and your wife are very welcome."

The doctor walks out and closes the door behind him. Jess walks over to his wife and his son. They just smile at each other, and Kathy holds the baby up. Jess takes hold of his son and cradles him in his arms. Jess is speechless at first.

Finally, with a big smile on his face, Jess utters the first words to his son, "Hello Joseph."

DATE - February 14th, 1973

San Francisco, CA

It is a cold and frosted Valentine's Day in San Francisco. An ambulance pulls into the emergency room drop off area at the San Francisco Regional Medical Center. William Shobe is the first one out of the back of the ambulance. William, a successful man in his late twenties, watches as the medical staff brings his pregnant wife, Becky, out of the ambulance on her gurney. William stands about 5'7" tall and holds a good build of 160 pounds with thinning brown hair and brown eyes. Becky is a petite, attractive 5'3" tall brunette with big brown eyes. A nurse comes up to William and helps him get dressed as Becky is taken into one of the delivery rooms. Once dressed, William enters the delivery room. The labor lasts only two hours when a baby's cry fills the delivery room. A nurse wraps the baby in a pink blanket. William smiles, realizing he has a daughter.

William looks at his wife, "You did good honey."

Becky breaks a smile, "I want to name her Kristen."

The nurse brings the baby over and hands the infant to Becky.

William smiles, "I like it." He looks at his daughter, "Hello Kristen. Welcome to the world."

DATE - April 6th, 1979
Alaskan Wilderness

It is a clear, cool early morning as the sun has started to break across the horizon. The light breeze carries the smell of pine and fresh snow to Joseph Thompson, a very mature six year old boy dressed in various animal skins and carrying a small bow on his back and an animal skin pouch slung across his left shoulder. Joseph is looking closely at the animal tracks in the snow. Joseph has been following the tracks for a couple miles now. The local tribe's best hunter, also dressed in various animal skins and carrying a knife and larger bow, has been teaching him how to track, hunt and survive off the land. This, however, is the first time they have gone out into the wilderness to apply what has been learned back at the village.

Joseph thinks for and minute and looks at the hunter, "Is it an elk?"

The hunter smiles and Joseph knows that he is right. Joseph also realizes that an elk is too large for him and his small bow to kill. The hunter will have to handle this one.

Joseph patiently tracks the animal for another hour. The hunter allows Joseph to lead the entire time, analyzing the young boy's every move. A little after an hour, the two of them spot the large elk at the bank of a river getting a drink of the cool, refreshing water. Joseph is in awe of the majestic animal, almost wishing they didn't have to kill such a fine creature to survive. Joseph slowly and quietly crawls into what he feels is the right position for the kill. The hunter follows Joseph into the position and does not correct him. Joseph knows he has done everything right so far. Once in position, the hunter takes aim with his bow being extra careful not to alert the animal of their presence. Joseph watches the hunter draw back his bow as he breathes in. The hunter slowly releases the air in his lungs and pauses. In the moments of pause, the hunter releases the deadly arrow. Joseph watches the arrow strike the elk and puts the elk down. Joseph smiles to himself as he realizes that he just completed his first hunt and track kill.

The hunter and Joseph walk over to the fallen animal. The hunter pulls out his knife. Joseph prepares himself for what he must do next. He knows the tribal custom of drinking the blood of the first animal killed on the person's first hunt. The hunter thrusts the knife into the animal. Joseph pulls out his tin cup from the pouch and fills it a third of the way with the elk's blood. Joseph looks at the hunter and then drinks the blood. The blood is thick and salty tasting, like nothing he has ever tasted before. Some of the blood runs down Joseph's chin. Once finished, Joseph gives a blood covered smile to the hunter.

The hunter speaks in broken English, "Now you are a true hunter."

Joseph takes in the hunter's words. The taste of blood and the thrill of the hunt is something that Joseph will never forget.

DATE - May 10th, 1979
Alaskan Wilderness

It is a dreary, overcast day with a slight mist in the air.
Joseph stands on a large rock in the middle of a small, clear, slow running river. He is holding the six foot long, wooden spear he made with both hands. He looks down into the crystal clear water and watches the fish swim around the edge of the rock, unaware he is there. Joseph takes a deep breath, taking in the smell of the fresh water, misty rain and fish. He raises the spear slowly. In a split second, he exhales and thrusts the spear down into the water. Joseph raises the spear, and to his surprise, finds that he has caught a fish. He takes the fish off the end of the spear and puts it in his animal skin pouch and prepares again.

Joseph repeats the steps many times over the next couple of hours. Although he misses many times, he manages to catch six fish. Remembering the words of his teacher about only killing what you need to survive, Joseph decides he has enough fish for the evening meal. He carefully makes his way across the six rocks that lead back to the bank of the river.

On the way back to camp, Joseph stops at a small grove of plants and berries. He looks each of them over carefully, trying to remember all that he was taught, so he can identify the edible ones. Joseph collects numerous plants and berries that are edible and not one that is dangerous.

Once Joseph gets back to the camp, he notices that the hunter has already started the fire and prepared the sleeping arrangements for the night. As the sun starts to set, Joseph prepares the fish and vegetation like he was taught. That night, by the soft glow of the fire, Joseph and the hunter eat a nice meal and then sleep.

DATE - June 4th, 1979
Alaskan Wilderness

It's a clear and somewhat warm early evening. The clear blue sky stretches on for what seems an eternity. The air is crisp and clean with a hint of pine and fresh water being carried on the light summer breeze. The hunter is sitting in the small camp when he hears something moving off to his left. The hunter glances over to see Joseph dropping the last of the materials he needs for the beaver trap. The hunter smiles to himself as he realizes Joseph was able to approach the camp without him hearing the boy, and that Joseph's training has been a success.

Over the next hour, the hunter watches Joseph work on building the beaver trap. Joseph concentrates hard on the construction of the trap, remembering everything he was told about if the trap is not perfect, the beaver will be able to escape and they will go hungry. He takes his time to make sure every detail is just right.

Once the trap is complete, the two of them grab their spears and set off for the river. Joseph leads them the two miles trough the incredibly green forest, brush and thicket. The two of them move slow as to not scare any of the wildlife which in turn could scare off the prey that they are looking to capture for dinner tonight.

Once they near the river, Joseph slowly moves the two of them into position to watch over the river. Joseph takes the trap and moves ever so carefully for the river while the hunter watches. Joseph quietly sets up the beaver trap and slowly works his way back over to the hunter, making sure not to disturb his surroundings.

Now all that is left to do is wait. The two of them lay motionless and observe the surroundings with their eyes, ears and nose. As the time passes, the hunter is impressed with Joseph's patience. The patience pays off as a beautiful looking beaver starts to approach the trap. The beaver takes the bait after a couple of minutes of sniffing around the trap. The trap falls and the beaver is caught.

Joseph smiles and whispers to the hunter, "I guess it is beaver tonight."

DATE - July 12th, 1979

Alaska

In the early morning hours of a beautiful summer day, Joseph and the hunter have been following some more elk tracks when they cross another set of tracks they both recognize right away.

Joseph looks at the hunter, "Those are bear tracks."

The hunter nods slowly, "Yes, a large bear. The tracks are fresh so the bear is near."

Joseph glances around, "What do we do now?"

The hunter scans the area, "We will backtrack for a mile and take another way around."

At that moment, they hear a deep growl and it is the sound of "it is too late". The two of them glance left and see the large bear staring at them. Neither of them make a sudden move. The hunter knows that the river is just 150 feet off to their right and the river is where they must go. Both of them take their spears with both hands and take a step to their right. The bear starts to move closer. The two of them sprint for the river and the bear closes quickly. They reach the rock bed just before the river, but the bear has caught up to them. The hunter turns to face the bear.

The bear swats at the hunter, but the hunter moves away and puts himself between Joseph and the bear.

The hunter thrusts his spear in and catches the bear in the left side. The bear cries out and swats again, but the hunter moves fast to get out of the way. Joseph just watches on in amazement at the hunter's skill. The hunter steps to his right and his foot slips on the rocks. The bear swats again and the hunter is knocked to the ground.

Joseph steps between the bear and the hunter. The bear stands up and Joseph's eyes widen. The bear stands at least ten feet tall. Joseph steps back and the rock under his foot gives out. Joseph falls to his back and cries out in pain as he lands on the rocks. Joseph raises his spear as the bear starts to drop down on him. Joseph closes his eyes, expecting to die. He hears the bear cry out. Joseph opens his eyes to see the bear laying next to him with his spear going into the heart of the bear.

Joseph jerks as the hunter grabs him and helps him to his feet. The hunter looks at the slain bear and then at Joseph who is shaking.

The hunter smiles, "You saved my life. Thank you."

After a few deep breaths, Joseph manages to speak, "What now?"

The hunter looks over to the bear, "We skin it, gather the meat and go home. The training is complete."

Joseph just stares at the bear, realizing what he was capable of doing. It's a lesson he will never forget.

DATE - August 18th, 1979
Alaska

Joseph and the hunter have only been back at the village for two days, but everyone has already heard the story about the bear. Not long after breakfast, the hunter comes and gets Joseph and his parents to take them to the village elder.

Joseph, Kathy, Jess and the hunter enter the elder's hut. The elder is sitting on the ground, facing the door. A fire burns in the middle of the hut. The four of them sit around the fire. The elder notices a bear claw hanging around Joseph's neck. The elder speaks in his native tongue.

The hunter translates, "He says that you are now at one with the land."

The elder speaks again and the hunter translates, "He says that you are very special and that your life-force is very strong."

Kathy and Jess look at their son. The elder speaks again. The hunter replies to the elder in native tongue. The elder nods his head and repeats his last statement.

The hunter translates, "He says that you were put on this Earth for a reason. That you are destined to change the world. That you will become legend and history will speak of you."

Joseph just stares at the elder. The elder nods and motions for them to leave. The four of them walk out of the elder's hut. Jess remembers the doctor saying his son was special and unique. Jess wonders if it could be true, could his son be destined for greatness? Jess knows that only time will tell.

Chapter 2

DATE - November 27th, 1979
Noctash, Alaska

Jess and Joseph are standing in the small delivery room waiting area in the local hospital. Kathy was rushed here when her pregnancy started having complications. The doctors have stabilized her now and proceeded with the birth, but Jess and Joseph were told to wait outside. Jess' face still has a look of worry, but he is confident in the small town's doctors. In fact, Jess has thought about it a lot and plans on moving his family to the town after the birth. Jess feels that Noctash, a nice quiet little town, would be a nice place to raise a family.

Jess and Joseph anxiously wait another hour, watching the other doctors and nurses casually going about their business.

Jess speaks in worry, "What could be taking so long?"

Joseph just looks up at his dad, not really sure of everything that is going on. Finally, the doctor comes out into the waiting room. He is an older gentleman in his mid-fifties and he has a smile on his face. The smile relaxes both Jess and Joseph.

The male doctor speaks calmly, "You have a healthy baby girl."

Joseph smiles in excitement, he was hoping for a baby sister. He tells himself right then that he is going to be the best big brother in the world.

Jess lets out a sigh of relief, "How's my wife?"

The doctor continues to smile, "She's fine. She would like the two of you to come in and see the baby."

The doctor pats Joseph on the head and takes notice of Joseph's bear claw necklace as Jess and Joseph walk by the doctor and into the room to be with Kathy and the newest member of the Thompson family.

DATE - March 12th, 1980
Noctash, Alaska

Joseph is walking through the snow covered town park on the way back to his house from the nearby stream where he fishes. He is carrying his homemade fishing pole in his right hand. Joseph lets his mind wander as he breathes in the fresh, crisp air and thinks about the day of fishing. Joseph is brought back to reality when he sees Brian Nelson. Brian is the local bully. He is a year older than Joseph and a little bigger than the other kids around their age and Brian likes to pick on any of the kids that he can. Some other kids playing in the park watch as Brian walks up to Joseph.

Brian stops about three feet in front of Joseph, "Give me that thing around your neck."

Joseph knows he is talking about the bear claw necklace. All the kids have talked about it since his family moved to town a few months ago.

Joseph shakes his head, "No way Brian."

Brian takes a step forward and balls up his hand into a fist, "Maybe you would like a black eye."

Joseph does the first thing to cross his mind, he drops his fishing pole and takes off running for home. Joseph looks back when he reaches the edge of the park to see if Brian is chasing him. Joseph watches as Brian breaks his fishing pole in half. Joseph turns and runs all the way home.

That same night, Kathy finishes cleaning the kitchen of the Thompson's small house after dinner. Kathy goes to play with their baby girl leaving Joseph and his dad in the living room alone.

Jess sits down in his recliner and opens his newspaper, "What happened to your fishing pole son? I didn't see it with the others."

Joseph continues to look at his book, "It's broke. I'll make another one tomorrow."

Jess closes the newspaper and sits forward in his chair knowing that there is a story behind the fishing pole, "How did it break?"

Joseph looks up at his father, "This kid named Brian broke it. He is always picking on the other kids. He wants my bear claw necklace."

Jess nods his head intently, "This Brian sounds like a bully, and it sounds like you have a problem. So, what are you going to do about it?"

Joseph shrugs, "I don't know dad. I know fighting is bad, but I don't want to lose my bear claw." Joseph pauses, "What should I do dad?"

Jess sits back, "You can't run from trouble your whole life son. You've got to stand up for what is right even if others do not agree with you. Remember, what you do

17

during the day, you have to sleep with at night. Sometimes son, you have to fight for what you feel is right." Jess smiles and opens the newspaper again, "Now, why don't you go play with your sister. You know how much she likes it and it will help take your mind off this."

Joseph closes his book and starts out of the room.

Joseph stops and turns back to his dad as Jess speaks again, "Remember this son, when the time comes, hit the other person first, hit them with everything you've got and never stop fighting until the fight is done."

Joseph walks out of the living room. He can't believe what his dad just said. Did his dad really say that it was okay to fight? Joseph plays with his sister for awhile, and then heads off to bed. Joseph thinks about what his dad said, especially the last words he spoke. He takes his dad's words to heart, and it is advice Joseph would never forget.

DATE - March 22nd, 1980
Noctash, Alaska

Joseph has been playing dodge ball and tag in the park all morning with some of his friends. It is a beautiful Alaskan day. The sun is shining and a light, cool breeze is blowing the crisp, clean air. During a break in the game, Joseph hears the crunching of ice and snow getting closer to him and he looks over to see Brian Nelson walking towards him. Joseph has managed to avoid Brian for the last ten days since the fishing pole incident, but it was obvious he was going to have to face him today. Joseph's heart beats faster and his breathing speeds up as Brian approaches.

Brian stops a few feet from Joseph, "Well, if it isn't the chicken. You gonna run again chicken or are you going to give me that bear claw?"

The words of his father run through Joseph's head. He can feel his blood start to get hot and his heart beats like a drum in his head. Joseph has had enough of Brian Nelson. Like being shot out of a gun, Joseph charges Brian and tackles Brian to the ground. Brian lands on his back with Joseph sitting on his chest. Joseph balls up his hands into fists and swings wildly at Brian's face. Brian starts flailing his arms, screaming and crying. Joseph hits Brian numerous times in the face. Joseph bloodies Brian's nose and blackens his left eye. All the kids gather around the two boys that are fighting and the kids start cheering Joseph on.

After a couple minutes, a middle aged oriental man runs up. The man is about 5'7" tall and weighs about 155 pounds. The oriental man looks to be in excellent shape for his age. The oriental man pulls Joseph off of Brian. As the oriental man checks to see if Brian is okay, Joseph panics and runs off.

Once the oriental man makes sure that Brian is okay, he looks around for Joseph, but all he sees are Joseph's tracks in the snow.

The oriental man looks at one of the boys standing nearby, "Do you know who the other boy was?"

The kid is not sure if he should answer the oriental man, but finally does, "His name is Joe, Joe Thompson."

The oriental man nods slightly at the young boy and looks back in the direction that Joseph ran off. The oriental man is not sure why, but he just has a feeling that he needs to find this, Joe Thompson, and find out more about the young boy.

DATE - April 14th, 1980

Noctash, Alaska

In the clear, cool Alaskan evening, Jess pulls his car up in front of a small, white house about two miles from their home. He puts the car in park and turns off the engine. Jess gets out of the driver's seat and Joseph gets out of the passenger's seat. Bundled up from the cold, they walk up to the front door and Jess knocks.

The oriental man from the park answers the door, "Hello Mr. Thompson. Won't you and your son come in."

Joseph recognizes the oriental man from the park. Joseph was excited when his father told him that Mr. Lee might be willing to teach him martial arts. The three of them walk into the living room which is decorated in an oriental motif. Mr. Lee sits in a recliner and Jess and Joseph sit on the small couch.

Mr. Lee speaks to Jess, "As I said before, I'm willing to teach your son if I think he is ready to start learning."

Jess replies, "Joseph is a good kid, and very smart for his age. I'm sure you'll be more than satisfied with him. Why don't I let the two of you talk and then you can let me know." Jess stands, "I'll wait in the car."

Jess walks out and Mr. Lee looks at Joseph, "That is a very unique necklace Joseph. What is it?"

Joseph clears his throat, "It's a bear claw."

Mr. Lee gets a surprised look, "Really, how did you get it?"

Joseph sits up, "I killed the bear on a hunting trip last year."

Mr. Lee sits forward in his chair, "Tell me about it."

Joseph tells him the story of the hunting trip and the bear. Mr. Lee sits quietly, listening to everything the young boy has to say. Once Joseph finishes the hunting story, he tells Mr. Lee about the fight with Brian Nelson. Mr. Lee is surprised at how intelligent and well schooled the young boy is. Mr. Lee can't help but think Joseph is different than the other kids he has met and refused to teach.

Once Joseph finishes the last story, he questions, "Is there anything else you want to hear about?"

Mr. Lee smiles and shakes his head, "No, those stories were good enough. It was very nice to meet you Joseph." Mr. Lee pauses and contemplates for a second, "I tell you what, why don't you come back tomorrow and if you want, we can begin your training."

Joseph jumps out of his chair in excitement, "Wow, thanks Mr. Lee! I'll tell my dad!"

Mr. Lee calmly stands and holds up his left hand. He puts his feet together and raises his right heel off the ground. He puts his right fist against the palm of his left hand which is flat. Both hands are held chest high. Mr. Lee bows his head down and back up. Joseph knows that the motion must have some meaning so he imitates the motion the best he can to Mr. Lee, then hurries out to tell his dad.

After Joseph leaves, a beautiful oriental woman in her late forties walks in, "You are going to teach him."

Mr. Lee nods, "Yes dear. I am."

Mrs. Lee questions, "Why him? You have refused everyone else."

Mr. Lee shrugs, "I don't exactly know why. Something tells me that Joseph is different. There is something special about that boy."

DATE - October 14th, 1980
Noctash, Alaska

Joseph stands in the corner of the 15 foot by 15 foot room in Mr. Lee's house. A 10 foot by 10 foot mat is on the floor in the middle of the room. Joseph is wearing a pair of sweatpants and a t-shirt. He watches as Mr. Lee, who is dressed in a traditional martial arts uniform, demonstrates on the homemade grappling dummy the different submission holds that Joseph will be learning today. Joseph can't believe how much he has learned in the time Mr. Lee has been training him. He has learned how to move, block and parry attacks. He has learned how to strike with his hands, elbows, feet and knees and he has learned various throws. Recently, he has started to learn grappling, ground fighting, submission and choke holds. He knows the future will bring pressure points and weapons training.

Joseph knows he has not mastered any of the techniques or philosophies he has studied, but he practices two hours a day, six days a week. Joseph devotes his Sundays to church and playing with his baby sister. He is trying to live up to his promise of being the best big brother in the world.

Joseph spends the next hour on the new techniques he was shown and the hour after that on old techniques. Mr. Lee is amazed at how fast Joseph learns. Once the session is over, Joseph bows to Mr. Lee and walks out of the room and into the living room.

As Joseph puts on his socks and running shoes, Mrs. Lee walks into the living room.

Mrs. Lee smiles, "Hello Joseph, how are you?"

Joseph smiles in return, he really likes Mrs. Lee, "I'm okay Mrs. Lee, just a little tired."

Mrs. Lee continues to straighten up the room, "Well, just be careful going home, okay."

Joseph nods and gives Mrs. Lee a hug, "I will."

Mrs. Lee watches as Joseph leaves. She is happy to see her husband so happy with teaching Joseph. It makes her feel bad that she cannot give him a son of his own. She is happy to see her husband treat Joseph as if he were their child. They both care for Joseph a lot.

DATE - February 19th, 1981
Noctash, Alaska

It is a wonderful Alaskan day. A light layer of snow covers the ground. The air is clear and crisp. The sun is shining and the sky is dotted with pure white clouds. Joseph is playing in the park with his sister and his best friend, Philip. Philip, who is the same age as Joseph, but slightly taller with light brown hair and hazel eyes, and Joseph look over to a group of kids standing around an older kid wearing a traditional martial arts uniform. The kid, who looks like an early teenager with black hair and brown eyes, is wearing a black belt.

Joseph looks at Philip, "Who is that kid?"

Philip replies, "That's Derek Gaines. He is one of the top students in my karate class. He is always showing off."

Derek, who is about five inches taller and 20 pounds heavier than Joseph, does a couple of kicks and then he spots Philip and Joseph. Derek walks over to them.

Derek looks at Joseph, "Is this the kid you've told me about Phil?"

Philip nods, "Yea. His name's Joe."

Derek smiles at Joseph, "I hear you're pretty good. What do you say, you want to spare some?"

Philip speaks up, "Come on Derek. Joe is only 8 and you are 13. It wouldn't be fair."

Derek smirks, "If he is as good as you say he is, then it shouldn't matter."

Joseph shakes his head, "I don't think so."

Joseph takes his sister's hand and they make their way home. Joseph feels good that he was able to walk away like he was taught, but he can't help but feel that he has not seen the last of Derek Gaines.

DATE - May 2nd, 1981
Noctash, Alaska

It is a beautiful spring Sunday in the small Alaskan town. A slight breeze blows the smell of pine through the town as the sun shines in the clear, blue sky. As church ends, Joseph and Philip head for the nearby ice cream shop. It is on the way home and they stop by there every Sunday after church. The rest of the Thompson family heads on home.

Joseph and Philip take about a half hour and enjoy their ice cream. Once the two boys are finished, they head off for Joseph's house. As the two boys approach the front yard, Joseph sees his sister playing with her dolls. She smiles when she sees her big brother.

Joseph smiles, "I'll be out as soon as I change sis."

Joseph goes inside to change and Philip goes over to play with Joseph's sister. Joseph puts on some sweatpants, a t-shirt and his running shoes. As Joseph walks out the front door, he sees Derek Gaines standing by his sister and Philip. Philip is laying on his back with a bloody nose and his sister is crying. Joseph sees one of his sister's dolls in Derek's left hand.

Derek looks at the little girl, "Shut up."

He pushes her to the ground with his right hand and rips the head off the doll. He drops the doll next to the little girl. Joseph has seen enough.

Joseph screams, "Derek!"

Derek looks over to see Joseph running at him. Derek smiles, takes his fighting stance and readies himself for Joseph. As Joseph gets to within arm's distance of Derek, Derek throws a straight right at Joseph's head. Joseph ducks under the punch and drives his right elbow into Derek's ribs. Derek takes a step back and prepares himself again.

Jess and Kathy run out the door to see what is happening. They see Joseph and Derek facing each other. Kathy starts towards the boys, but Jess grabs her arm.

Kathy looks at Jess, "Do something."

Jess stares over at his son, "Just a second."

Derek throws a left hook at Joseph. Joseph catches the arm with his right hand, drives his left hand into Derek's left shoulder, steps back and throws Derek to the ground. Derek rolls a couple times, scrambles to his feet and gets back in his fighting stance. Joseph takes his fighting stance. Derek throws a roundhouse kick with his right leg. Joseph ducks under the leg and dives into Derek's left leg and tackles him to the ground. Joseph sits on Derek's chest in a mount position like he was trained and punches Derek in the face, twice with his right fist and once with his left.

Derek panics, not knowing what to do. He rolls over to his stomach and tries to stand up. Joseph wraps his legs around Derek's waist. Joseph slides his right arm around Derek's throat, grabbing his left bicep and placing his left hand on the back of Derek's head. Joseph shifts his weight to his right and they roll back to the ground as Joseph starts choking Derek.

Jess realizes that now is the time to stop the fight. Jess runs over to the two boys and pulls them apart. Derek scrambles to his feet and runs off crying. His bloody nose and lip are nothing compared to his bruised ego. Joseph stands up and starts taking deep breaths to calm himself down.

Kathy hurries over to Jess and the others, "Is everyone okay?"

Joseph nods, "I'm okay mom."

Philip stands up and wipes his nose, "I'm okay Mrs. Thompson, just a bloody nose."

Kathy looks over to see her daughter standing and hugging Joseph's right leg. Kathy takes Philip inside to take care of his nose.

Jess looks at his son, "That was a very noble thing you did son."

Jess pats Joseph on the head and walks back inside.

Joseph gets on his knees next to his sister, "I love you sis. No one will ever hurt you while I'm around."

She gives him a big hug and manages to say, "I love you."

The two of them spend the rest of the day playing together. That night Joseph would reply the fight in his head. The fight makes him realize how powerful his training could be. He vows that he will only use his training to help others who cannot fight for themselves. He drifts off to sleep, proud of the fact that he protected his sister.

DATE - January 27th, 1982
Noctash, Alaska

It has been a bad winter so far with lots of snow and ice. This day has been no different. The temperature has dropped below zero and the snow continues to fall. Joseph stayed the weekend with Mr. and Mrs. Lee because his parents and sister went to Hughes. They are suppose to pick him up at the Lee's house at 5 pm.

Joseph is sitting on the couch in the living room and he looks at the clock on the wall. It is now 6 pm and he starts to worry. Mr. Lee watches on, wanting to say something to help calm the boy, but he too is starting to worry. The two of them sit anxiously for another half hour when they hear a knock at the front door. Joseph grabs his things as Mr. Lee answers the door. Mr. Lee opens the door to see the sheriff standing there.

The sheriff, a heavy man in his early forties, speaks, "Mr. Lee, is Joseph Thompson here?"

Mr. Lee nods, "Yes, please come in."

Joseph drops his things when the sheriff walks into the living room. He knows something is wrong. Mr. Lee sits on the couch next to where Joseph is standing and the sheriff stands next to the recliner. Joseph continues to stand.

The sheriff speaks, "Joseph, I'm sorry, but I have some very bad news. I'm not really sure how to say this." He pauses, "Your parents and sister were in a car wreck just a few miles outside of town."

Mr. Lee sighs, "Dear God."

Joseph swallows and tries to hold back the tears, "Are they okay? Where are they?"

The sheriff looks at Mr. Lee and back at Joseph. Joseph knows the answer by the look on the sheriff's face and the first few tears start to roll down Joseph's cheeks.

The sheriff speaks as consoling as possible, "I'm sorry, but the three of them died in the wreck."

Joseph can't hold it in anymore and the tears flow. Joseph runs out of the room. Mr. Lee gets up and starts after Joseph. Joseph runs out the back door and is halfway across the snow covered back yard when Mr. Lee catches him. Mr. Lee wraps his arms around Joseph and holds him tight.

Joseph is crying and squeezing Mr. Lee tight, "Why? Why did they have to die?"

Mr. Lee sighs, "I don't know Joseph. All I know is that everything happens for a reason."

Joseph sniffles, "I'll never see them again. I'm all alone now."

Mr. Lee shakes his head, leans back and looks into Joseph's eyes, "That's not true. They will always be in your mind and your heart. You can visit them anytime." He pauses, "And I know they will watch over you from heaven now that they are with God. So, they are never really gone."

Joseph buries his face in Mr. Lee's chest, "There is no God. God would not let this happen."

Mr. Lee sighs and holds Joseph tight. Mrs. Lee comes out and she too hugs Joseph tight. Neither one knows what to say to the boy. All they can do is pray that Joseph will be okay.

DATE - August 2nd, 1982
Noctash, Alaska

Mr. and Mrs. Lee enter the Noctash City Hall building for what should be the last time in the adoption process. Mr. Lee and his wife were happy that Joseph was okay with their adopting him. They told him that he would keep the name Thompson, just they would become his legal guardians and parents.

They also told Joseph that they plan on moving to San Francisco, California. Joseph didn't seem to mind that either. Mr. Lee is still worried about Joseph. He has noticed that Joseph has buried himself in his training, but that he has not gone to church since the funeral. Mr. Lee knows that only time will tell how Joseph will heal. Mr. and Mrs. Lee walk into the county clerk's office.

The clerk hands Mr. Lee a packet of papers, "Keep these papers in a safe place. We will have a copy of all the paperwork on file here if something ever happens to your original copy."

Mr. Lee nods, "Thank you."

The clerk smiles, "I will contact the children's home to let them know everything is complete and that you are on your way over."

Mr. Lee bows his head and Mr. and Mrs. Lee walk out. They get in their car and head for the children's home to get Joseph and take him home.

Chapter 3

DATE - October 3rd, 1982
San Francisco, CA

Joseph continues to look out the window of the car at the huge city as they cross the Golden Gate Bridge on their way to their new home. Mr. and Mrs. Lee told Joseph that they would be near Lake Merced and close to the Pacific Ocean. Joseph liked the idea that he would still be able to go fishing. He is already enrolled in his new school. Joseph is ready to meet some new kids and make new friends.

Joseph can't believe how big and noisy the city is as they continue down 19th Avenue. He notices that it looks like everyone is so busy and has something to do. Joseph shakes his head as everything seems to move so much faster here. It looks like there is a million things to do in this city. Joseph smiles at his new surroundings. It is the first time he has smiled in a long time. Joseph can't wait to explore this new place. Joseph is completely taken by his new home.

Jody Slyman

DATE - February 14th, 1983
San Francisco, CA

Joseph is sitting at his desk in his classroom. Joseph puts the finishing touches on his Valentine's Day card, however, he has no idea who he is going to trade with. There are an equal number of girls and boys in the class, but he hasn't made friends with any of them yet. Some of the other kids have asked about his bear claw necklace, but he hasn't talked to anyone about his past yet. He doesn't want to tell just anyone about his training and his family, he wants to make sure it is the right person.

A few minutes later, a girl places a Valentine's Day card on his desk. Joseph looks up at the girl from his seat. He immediately sees how pretty the young girl is. She has shoulder length dark brown hair and incredible blue eyes. She has on a nice white and yellow dress with a ribbon in her hair. Joseph likes her immediately.

The girl smiles at Joseph, "Hi, I'm Kristen."

Joseph smiles back, "I'm Joseph."

Kristen slides her card towards Joseph, "Would you like to trade cards with me?"

Joseph holds out his card to Kristen, "Sure, that would be great."

Kristen takes Joseph's card and returns to her seat. Joseph looks at the card Kristen made. A couple minutes later, Joseph looks over to see Kristen smiling at him. He returns the smile. That day, Kristen and Joseph spend the entire recess talking to each other. Joseph doesn't tell her everything, just a few little things about where he is from.

Once school is over, they each head home to tell their parents about their new friend. As Joseph climbs into bed that night, he can't help but think that Kristen and him will be good friends. Little does Joseph know that Kristen is thinking the very same thing that night.

DATE - February 24th, 1983
San Francisco, CA

Papa Martoni, a well dressed man in his fifties that stands around 6'3" tall and weighs close to 240 pounds with black hair and brown eyes, walks into the dining room of his incredibly large and well protected home. He takes a seat at the table. His breakfast is waiting for him just the way he likes it. The morning paper sits next to his plate. Papa Martoni smiles as he reads the top headline: "DEATH OF FRANCISCO CARUZZI RULED AS ACCIDENT".

Papa Martoni knows that he now owns all the business in San Francisco. He thinks about the long road that finally lead to this day. A young man in a nice blue suit walks in and stands a couple feet to the right of Papa Martoni.

Papa Martoni slides the paper to the man, "Good work. Get the others. We will hold a meeting in one hour."

The man nods and leaves the room. As Papa Martoni finishes his breakfast, he plans his next move. He thinks to himself, it is time to turn up the heat on the independent operators. Yes he thinks, it is time for blood to be shed.

DATE - March 5th, 1983
San Francisco, CA

On a clear, cool day in the city an unmarked Dodge Diplomat pulls up to the taped off crime scene in an alley just off Franklin Street. Detective Darius Jackson, a black man in his early thirties, gets out of the car. He stands around

6'1" tall and weighs in at a well built 215 pounds. He has caught quite a bit of lip since becoming the first black detective in his department. However, he was assigned to follow the Martoni family and no doubt this was their work. It is the third murder scene in the last two weeks.

Detective Jackson walks over to another detective who is standing near a trash dumpster, "So, what exactly do we have?"

The detective looks at him, "Two more bodies. Each had their hands tied and each had one bullet put in their heads."

Detective Jackson shakes his head and looks down at the bodies, "Another execution. Were these two into anything?"

The detective nods, "They were into opium, but they didn't work for any organization that I'm aware of. It looks like the Martoni family is branching out."

Detective Jackson nods, "Now with the Caruzzi family out of the way, all that is left is the independents. It looks like they are the next target of the Martoni family. Make sure whatever you have makes it to my office."

The detective nods and walks off. Detective Jackson slowly walks around the dumpster and the bodies, then he walks up and down the alley taking in everything. He can't help but think that more bodies will be coming soon.

DATE - February 16th, 1984
San Francisco, CA

It is a cool, but clear day in the city. A slight breeze is on the air and the usual noises of the city can be heard. Joseph and Kristen are sitting and talking by the fence during recess. They have spent almost every day together. The two of them have become the best of friends. Joseph has just finished telling Kristen about what happened to his parents and sister back in Alaska.

Kristen hugs him and gives him a kiss on the cheek, "I'm so sorry about your family Joseph."

Joseph looks down, "It still bothers me some, but I try my best not to think about it."

Kristen smiles and trying to cheer him up, she changes the subject, "So, when are you going to tell me about your necklace?"

Joseph shrugs, "Someday. I'll tell you what it means to me though."

Kristen playfully pushes his shoulder, "Well, what is it?"

Joseph looks at her and replies with a serious tone, "As long as I wear it, I know I can do anything I put my mind to."

Kristen lets out a playful laugh, but she knows Joseph is serious. She admires Joseph's strength and independence. Joseph admires Kristen's ability to care and love with no strings attached. It is obvious to both that they are getting closer.

DATE - April 8th, 1984
San Francisco, CA

It's a cool, clear mid-morning with a slight breeze blowing. Mr. Lee walks into his kitchen. Joseph is out for his morning run and Mrs. Lee is working in the yard. Mr. Lee sits down at the kitchen table and picks up the newspaper that is laying there. The top headline stands out: "TWO MORE BODIES FOUND EXECUTED".

Mr. Lee takes a deep breath, shakes his head and puts the paper down. He can't help but think to himself if he should have brought his wife and Joseph to San Francisco with all of the violence that has been going on. He never really could explain his full reason for moving. He just had a gut feeling that it was time to move and it also just felt like San Francisco was the place to go. Mr. Lee clears his head and convinces himself that the police will handle this violence.

DATE - March 10th, 1985
San Francisco, CA

It is a beautiful, spring like afternoon with a warming sun and a light breeze. Kristen is sitting on one of the swings on the school playground. The playground is full of kids laughing, playing and just having fun. Kristen is waiting for Joseph who had to talk to their teacher before recess.

Bobby Kerns, a brown haired boy from their class, walks over to Kristen, "Would you like me to push you?"

Kristen doesn't want to be mean, but shakes her head, "No that's okay. I'm waiting on Joseph."

Bobby lowers his head and walks off. Kristen knows that Bobby likes her, but she doesn't have any real feelings towards him. She feels bad for Bobby because he keeps trying to be close to her and she has to keep saying no to him. Kristen has noticed that he doesn't try to get real close to any of the other girls in their class. However, her mind clears and Kristen smiles as Joseph comes running up.

Joseph walks around behind her and pulls the swing back a couple of feet, "Are you ready?"

Kristen nods and starts to giggle, "Yes."

Joseph lets go and Kristen starts swinging. Bobby Kerns watches on from over by the tornado slide. He can't help but feel rejected and all he wants is to be in Joseph's place. Joseph continues to push Kristen completely unaware of all the kids around them. Kristen just keeps laughing and smiling. She loves all the fun they have together.

DATE - May 21st, 1985
San Francisco, CA

Most citizens are out enjoying the warm, clear spring night, but Detective Jackson is sitting at his desk in his very neatly organized office area. This is where he has found himself almost every night for as long as he can remember. Detective Jackson looks over the paperwork and pictures from the recent crime scene. He shakes his head in frustration, three more bodies and the number just keeps rising. He knows that the evidence must be solid and so far they have not been able to connect any of the bodies to Papa Martoni. That fact makes Detective Jackson very upset.

Detective Jackson continues to flip through folders full of paperwork and glancing through what seems like a never ending stack of pictures over the next hour. He sits back, rubs his eyes and looks at his watch to see that it is 10:30 pm. Detective Jackson decides to call it a night and get a fresh start in the morning. He opens the bottom right drawer on his desk to expose a large stack of case files. He piles the current paperwork on top and closes the drawer. He turns off his desk lamp. As Detective Jackson walks to his car, he can't help but think that something in the case has to break soon.

DATE - April 28th, 1986

Jody Slyman

San Francisco, CA

Kristen is sitting at a picnic table in the park near her home on what is a perfect spring day. The temperature is just right with a soft blowing breeze. She is wearing a baggy t-shirt, gym shorts and tennis shoes and has a gym bag sitting next to her. Kristen can't believe that she and Joseph are in Junior High now. They only have a couple of classes together, but she loves all the time outside of school that they spend with each other. Kristen knows that the time is getting close as to when her and Joseph usually meet at the park once Joseph is done with his homework and training for the day.

Kristen just sits and waits patiently for Joseph and in about ten more minutes, he comes jogging up. They hug and kiss each other on the cheek.

Kristen pulls a basketball, her favorite sport, out of the gym bag, "So, are you ready for your whipping?"

Joseph smiles at her, "Bring it on girl."

The two of them walk over to the nearby basketball court. They play some basketball for about an hour in which Kristen runs circles around Joseph.

The two of them decide to take a break and they sit back down at the picnic table.

Kristen jokes with Joseph, "So, were you trying or are you just that bad?"

Joseph smiles and nods his head, "Okay, so basketball is not my game."

Kristen smiles and just stares a Joseph, then brings up another subject that she is still wanting to know about, "So, is today the day you tell me about your necklace?"

Joseph doesn't say anything and just lets out a slight laugh. Joseph's response makes Kristen realize that she is not going to find out about the necklace today. They have

38

known each other for some time now and she really wants to know the story behind the necklace, but she also knows about Joseph's family back in Alaska and she doesn't want to push too hard in case the story is a hurtful one as well.

The two of them talk for a little while longer until Kristen's dad shows up to take her home. Once Kristen and her dad drive off, Joseph runs off for his house. In bed that night, Joseph dreams about Kristen and little does he know that Kristen is dreaming about him.

DATE - June 8th, 1986
San Francisco, CA

In the heat of the early summer night, two young men, no more than 25 years old, are standing in a dark alley awaiting their buyer. Each young man is wearing a t-shirt, baggy jeans and a bandana to signify the gang that they belong to. One of the young men has a backpack slung over his right shoulder.

Three men dressed in nice suits approach the two young men from behind. The three men recognize their targets right away. The two young men never see the three men approach. The three men in suits each pull out a 9mm pistol. They stop about 30 feet behind the two young men.

All three men raise their pistols at the same time. Twenty shots ring out, joining the rest of the noise of the city night, and the two young men fall dead in a pool of blood. The three men quickly retreat back down the alley to a waiting car and disappear into the streets.

The two dead bodies would become the next set of paperwork in the Martoni case. A body count that continues to rise.

DATE - May 14th, 1987

After dinner at the Shobe household, Joseph and Kristen are laying on the floor in Kristen's nice sized living room. Kristen has already changed into her pajama shorts and t-shirt and Joseph is wearing a pair of jean shorts and a t-shirt. The two of them are watching TV. Kristen slowly moves her hand over and pokes Joseph in the side.

Joseph smiles, "I wouldn't do that."

A minute later, Kristen pokes Joseph again. Joseph rolls over to face Kristen.

Kristen smiles and speaks quickly, "Don't even think about it."

Joseph gives her a sly look, "Okay."

Then, Joseph quickly pokes Kristen in the side. The two of them start wrestling around on the floor. It doesn't take long and Kristen finds herself on her back with her arms pinned to the floor. Joseph is laying on top of her and the two of them are laughing.

William Shobe comes walking in to see what is going on, "Well, it looks like he got you again Kristen. Of course, you should expect it with all the training he's had."

Kristen loves the fact that her parents approve so much of Joseph. She likes the fact that Mr. and Mrs. Lee approve so much of her. Joseph tickles Kristen for a few seconds, then stands up and helps her up.

Kristen catches her breath, "One of these days I'll get you."

Joseph smiles and looks at his watch, "It's getting late, I have to be going."

Becky walks into the room, "Well, it was nice to see you again Joe."

William smiles, "Be careful going home."

Joseph nods, "I will, and thanks again for dinner Mr. and Mrs. Shobe."

Kristen walks him out. They stand on the porch and stare into each other's eyes for a few seconds, then they hug. Joseph kisses Kristen on the forehead, turns and walks off. Kristen walks back in to see her parents smiling at her.

Kristen smiles and quickly walks pass them, "We're just good friends. Okay."

William replies sarcastically as he looks at Becky, "Oh, that's what it's called these days."

Kristen was right, she and Joseph have never talked about going steady. However, neither of them have ever gone steady with anyone else.

DATE - July 19th, 1987
San Francisco, CA

Papa Martoni sits in his favorite chair and watches as the other members of his organization leave his den after their evening meeting. The update is just what he wanted to hear. He thinks about the detective that is trying to build a case against him. His sources on the inside have kept him updated on every step Detective Jackson takes. Papa Martoni thinks about what his father told him. The words are as clear in his head now as when his father spoke the words to him, "If you have money and power, you can manipulate the system and make it work for you."

Right now, the Martoni family has plenty of both. Papa Martoni gets up and walks over to the window as the sun starts to set. Papa Martoni smiles as he thinks about how everyone fears his family. He thinks about how fear has become his most powerful ally. Never having to face fear himself, Papa Martoni does not know how powerful fear really is.

Chapter 4

DATE - June 17th, 1988
San Francisco, CA

It is a beautifully warm summer day. The sky is clear and a breeze is blowing just enough to keep the heat down to a bearable level. The usual sounds of the city echo in the distance as Joseph and Kristen are taking a walk through the park. Kristen is wearing sandals, tight fitting jean shorts and a tight fitting tank top. Joseph is wearing sandals, baggy shorts and a loose fitting t-shirt. Kristen and Joseph have just completed their first year of High School. They both can't believe how different High School was, but now they have all summer together.

Joseph speaks, "You did really good in basketball this year."

Kristen takes hold of his hand, "Thanks. By the way, how's your training going?"

Joseph shrugs, "Fine I guess. Also, my mom and dad would like you to come over for dinner again sometime."

Kristen smiles, "I'd like that."

They continue to walk, talk and enjoy the wonderful summer day. After they finish walking through the park,

Joseph walks Kristen home. They hug each other and Kristen gives him a kiss on the cheek.

Kristen smiles, "So, I guess I'll see you tomorrow."

Joseph nods, "I can be over around noon if you want to have lunch together."

Kristen slowly lets go of Joseph's hand, "Sounds good to me."

Kristen goes inside and Joseph walks home. The whole way home, all Joseph can think about is how wonderful Kristen is. He knows that there is no way he would ever let anything happen to her.

Joseph thinks to himself, "I'll protect her better than I did my sister."

DATE - August 11th, 1988
San Francisco, CA

Detective Jackson is sitting at his desk, unaware of all the lunch time commotion going on around him. He puts down his cup of coffee and continues to read over the latest paperwork from the last crime scene. He has spent the last two days going over the recent evidence and he believes he has found something to link Papa Martoni to at least one murder. If the informant's information pays off, it could be the break in the case he was looking for.

The captain, a man in his late forties, walks up, "How is the case going detective?"

Detective Jackson sits back, "It's better today than yesterday. I think I might have found the break I was looking for. I'm going to talk to an informant this evening to see what he has to offer."

The captain nods, "Just make sure everything is airtight. You know as well as I do that the District Attorney will not go near the Martoni family unless it is an open and shut case."

Detective Jackson nods in return, "That is exactly what I'm trying to do. I have plenty of evidence, all I need is the link to the Martoni family."

The captain gives a slight nod, "Well, keep me posted."

Detective Jackson returns to his paperwork, "No problem captain."

Detective Jackson looks through the pictures with great enthusiasm, but he still knows that he must take his time. The captain is right, he knows that the case must be airtight before going to the District Attorney with it, but he knows he is getting closer. Detective Jackson also wants it to be an open and shut case with no bumps.

DATE - July 30th, 1989
San Francisco, CA

It is a sultry summer night in the big city. It is hot and humid, but that hasn't kept all the teenagers from coming out for the night. The air is thick with the noise of cars and blasting radios. Joseph and Kristen are parked at the local Sonic. Kristen is once again showing off her incredible body with her tight jean shorts and tank top. Joseph is wearing his usual baggy shorts and loose fitting t-shirt. They are waiting for the food to arrive. Kristen loves Joseph's car. It is a 1966 Pontiac GTO convertible with a 389 with two 4 barrel carburetors and a 4 speed transmission. It is painted a beautiful silver blue color.

Joseph looks over at Kristen, "Another good year for basketball."

Kristen nods, "Yep."

Joseph smiles, "So, I guess you'll try out for varsity next year?"

Kristen shrugs, "I don't know. Varsity is a big step and I don't think I'm good enough."

Joseph gets a surprised look, "Are you kidding? You are one of the best on the team."

Kristen kind of smiles, "On the Junior Varsity team. Varsity is completely different. I just don't know if I could do it."

Joseph turns in his seat to face Kristen, "You know, back in Alaska, I was tested so many times. Each time I wasn't sure if I would be able to pass the next test, but I managed." Joseph pauses for a second, "I killed a ten foot bear when I was six years old. That's how I got this necklace."

Joseph tells Kristen the story of the hunting trip and the encounter with the bear. Kristen just listens in amazement. She is speechless. About that time, the food and drinks arrive and Joseph pays for them. He hands Kristen her food and drink. They talk a little about school and what to expect from the upcoming year. Once they finish their food, Joseph drives Kristen home. He pulls up in front of her house.

Kristen looks at Joseph, "Thanks for dinner."

She unbuckles her seatbelt and opens the door to get out.

Joseph grabs her arm, "Wait." He takes the bear claw necklace from around his neck, "I want you to have this."

Kristen gets a surprised look, "I can't take your necklace. It means so much to you."

Joseph leans over and ties it around her neck, "I insist. Besides, I don't think I need it anymore." Joseph sits back, "Just remember what I told you about this necklace, as long as I was wearing it, I felt like I could do anything."

Kristen gives him a big hug, "Thank you Joseph. I'll take good care of it and I'll always wear it."

Joseph smiles, "What can I say? I care about you."

Kristen smiles and kisses Joseph quickly on the lips, "I care about you too."

Kristen gets out of the car and rushes inside. Joseph drives home and the whole way he can't quit smiling and thinking about how nice the brief kiss was.

DATE - September 9th, 1989
San Francisco, CA

Papa Martoni is sitting in his favorite chair in his den after finishing his lunch. Papa Martoni's son, Varges, is sitting on the leather couch with his friend Daniel. Varges, a man in his early twenties, stands about 6'1" tall and weighs around 210 pounds. He has black hair and hazel eyes. Varges is dressed in a nice gray suit and he carries a 9mm pistol in a shoulder holster under his right shoulder. Daniel, who is also in his early twenties, stands around 5'11" tall and weighs close to 200 pounds. He has brown hair and brown eyes. Daniel is wearing a blue suit and carries his 9mm pistol in a shoulder holster under his left shoulder. Papa Martoni's lawyer, a distinguished looking man in his fifties, walks into the den.

The lawyer sits in a chair near Papa Martoni, "I have everything under control. We have nothing to worry about. Just keep everyone cool on the stand and I'll take care of the rest."

Papa Martoni nods not feeling real sure about his lawyer, "How does the case look?"

The lawyer smiles, "They have nothing. I'll poke holes in all their evidence and witnesses."

Papa Martoni sits forward, "This is my life and my family we are talking about so I have a backup plan in place."

The lawyer stands, nods and leaves. He knows better than to ask about the plan.

Papa Martoni looks at his son with a very serious look, "You know what to do. Make sure it happens."

Varges smiles, "Consider it done Papa."

Varges and Daniel stand and walk out of the room.

DATE - October 12th, 1989
San Francisco, CA

In the darkness of the city night, the incredible commotion of the city is completely unaware of the incident that is unfolding in a dark alley. A middle-aged man in ragged clothing kneels next to a trash dumpster. His hands are tied behind his back. Varges and Daniel are standing just a few feet away from the man.

Varges pulls out his 9mm pistol with his left hand, "Nobody talks about my father."

The man's eyes widen, "I wasn't going to say a thing. I just told the detective that to get him off my back. I wasn't even going to show up at the trial."

Daniel smiles, "We're here to make sure of that."

Varges takes aim, "Nothing personal, this is just business."

Varges pulls the trigger. The single shot to the head sends the man to the ground.

Daniel looks at Varges, "Our first hit, how does it feel?"

Varges smiles as he puts his pistol away, "Feels like I'm really one of the family now." Varges looks over to Daniel, "Lets get out of here and celebrate with a drink."

Daniel nods his approval, "Sounds good to me."

The two young men walk off talking about their first hit and the hopes of many more to come.

DATE - October 14th, 1989
San Francisco, CA

The District Attorney, an attractive woman in her forties wearing a blue female suit, is sitting at the prosecutor's table in a courtroom packed with news crews and citizens. The Assistant District Attorney, a man in his forties wearing a gray suit, is sitting next to her. The Assistant DA turns around and starts whispering to Detective Jackson who is sitting in the front row.

The judge grabs his gavel with great impatience, "Since the DA cannot produce their eyewitness, I have no choice but to grant the defense's motion." He slams down the gavel, "This case is dismissed."

The Assistant DA turns back around. Detective Jackson can't believe it. He had an open and shut case, but his informant never showed up. A female uniformed police officer walks up and hands Detective Jackson a piece of paper. Detective Jackson reads the piece of paper, but he can't believe what it says.

The DA turns around to Detective Jackson, "What is it detective?"

Detective Jackson speaks with a little disgust, "My informant has been found. It appears he has been executed."

The DA shakes her head, "Papa Martoni wins again. You know, one day we are going to finally get him."

Detective Jackson crumples the paper, "I'll get started on the case files again."

The DA and Assistant DA gather their things and walk out of the courtroom.

Papa Martoni stops near Detective Jackson on the way out of the courtroom, "Don't look too upset. You should be happy the system worked the way it is suppose to."

Detective Jackson responds, "You may have gotten passed being judged by your peers, but mark my words, nobody is above the law. Your day of judgment will come again and I hope I'm there to see it."

Papa Martoni smiles, "Well, better luck next time."

Detective Jackson watches as Papa Martoni walks out of the courtroom triumphantly. Detective Jackson shakes his head, feeling like he let the city down. He only hopes that something even worse doesn't happen because of this.

DATE - July 4th, 1990
San Francisco, CA

On a clear, hot holiday night, Varges and Daniel walk out of a night club where they have been celebrating the holiday. They both have a beer in their hand. A nearby police officer watches the two young men walk to their car which is parked in an isolated spot on a nearby parking lot. As Daniel pulls the keys out of his pocket to unlock the door, the police officer walks up behind the two young men.

The police officer speaks, "I see you boys have been doing some drinking."

Varges and Daniel turn around to see the officer standing there. They also see that he is alone.

Daniel responds in a cheerful manner, "A little, but not much officer."

The officer nods slightly, "I'm going to need to see some identification."

Varges smiles, "No problem officer."

Varges reaches into his jacket like he is reaching for his inside pocket, but instead of an ID card, Varges pulls out his pistol. The police officer, who had his hand lightly touching his pistol, goes for his gun. The police officer draws his gun a bit too late. Three shots later, the officer lays in a pool of blood from a shot to the neck.

Daniel looks around to see if anyone saw what just happened.

Varges puts his pistol away, "Any witnesses?"

Daniel tips his beer to Varges, "Not a one."

Varges and Daniel get in their car and drive off.

DATE - November 14th, 1990
San Francisco, CA

Joseph, wearing jeans and a sweatshirt, is sitting about halfway up the second set of bleachers in their High School gym. The gym is packed full of students, faculty and family as one of the year's big games starts to draw to an end. Joseph watches as Kristen makes a perfect three point shot to give her team the lead. The game continues to go back and forth, but when the game finally ends, it ends in a victory. The varsity team joins in a circle in the middle of the court and says a cheer. As all the players start heading for the locker room, Kristen looks around and finds Joseph in the crowd. She winks and waves at him. Joseph smiles and waves back. As Kristen jogs off the court, Joseph notices the bear claw hanging around her neck.

Joseph makes his way out of the gym and to the parking lot. He puts his coat on as he waits by his car for about half an hour when Kristen, wearing tight blue jeans, long sleeve shirt and coat, finally comes out to Joseph's car. The two of them get in the GTO and they head to the local McDonald's for dinner. Joseph gets their food and they take a seat in one of the booths.

Kristen looks across the booth at Joseph, "I can't thank you enough for all the support you've given me."

Joseph gets lost in her sky blue eyes for a moment and finally speaks, "I'm just glad to see you so happy."

Joseph takes a few bites not understanding the feelings that have just come over him. He can feel his heart beat faster when Kristen looks at him. The two of them carry on the usual school and sports conversation as they finish their meal.

With the meal done, Joseph drives Kristen home. He parks his car in front of her house and walks her up to the front door.

Kristen hugs him tight, "Thanks for being so wonderful."

Joseph hugs her and the words just come out, "I love you."

Kristen steps back and gives him a little surprised look, "I love you too."

An uneasy quiet comes between them and Kristen finally speaks, "I better get inside."

Joseph smiles, "I'll see you tomorrow."

Kristen opens the door and goes inside. Joseph walks back to his car, gets in and drives home. The whole way home he can't figure out why he said it. It finally hits him as Joseph pulls up to his house, the feelings have been there all along. It just finally got to be more than he could hold in.

DATE - December 25th, 1990
San Francisco, CA

It is a wonderfully white Christmas Day in the city. A light layer of snow covers the ground and the temperature has dropped below freezing. Kristen, wearing her blue jeans and a Christmas sweatshirt with her shoulder length brown hair pulled back into a ponytail and as always, the bear claw necklace, is sitting next to the Christmas tree in the living room and her parents are sitting on the couch. A small fire burns in the fireplace.

Kristen opens her presents with her mom and dad. She can't wait until Joseph and his parents arrive. She has thought a lot about the words they spoke. She didn't realize how much she cared for Joseph until that night. The last month and a half she has felt awkward around him. Then, the doorbell rings.

Kristen gets up and answers the door, "Hello Mr. and Mrs. Lee." She looks and smiles at Joseph who is also wearing jeans and a Christmas sweatshirt, "Hello Joseph. Come on in."

She gives Mr. and Mrs. Lee a hug and then she awkwardly hugs Joseph and gives him a kiss on the cheek. All the adults are smiling at the two of them.

The six of them make their way to the dining room where a nice meal is waiting for them. The four adults sit down at the table, leaving the only two open seats next to each other. Joseph pulls Kristen's chair out and she sits down. Joseph sits down next to her. It is an uneventful dinner. The conversation is mainly about work and school. They talk about college plans. Once dinner is done, the six of them make their way into the living room where the fire is burning and Christmas music plays in the background. The six of them visit for about another hour, then Joseph and his parents get up to leave. Joseph doesn't realize he is standing under the mistletoe.

Becky looks at Kristen, "Well Kristen, I think something is needed here."

Joseph and Kristen both look up. Kristen smiles, steps forward and kisses Joseph. The kiss seals the feelings. It is a nice, lingering kiss. The four adults look at each other and smile. Once the kiss is over, Joseph and his parents make their way to the door. Kristen watches as Joseph leaves. Once Joseph and his parents are gone, she goes to her room and pulls out her old diary. All she can write about is how wonderful Joseph is.

DATE - February 14th, 1991
San Francisco, CA

It's a cold, clear night with patches of snow and ice covering the ground. For the last three hours, the Shobe's house has hosted a birthday party for Kristen. Now the party is over and everyone has left except for Joseph. Kristen, in her jeans, t-shirt, birthday hat and bear claw necklace, is picking up paper plates from the kitchen table and throwing them away. Joseph, having just put on his jacket, pulls out a single red rose and walks up behind Kristen. Kristen gets a surprised look on her face when she turns around and sees the rose.

Joseph smiles, "Happy birthday Kristen."

Joseph hands her the rose and kisses her on the cheek. Kristen is speechless.

Joseph steps back, "I should be going. It's getting late."

Kristen smiles and finally responds, "I'll see you tomorrow."

Joseph gives a quick nod of his head and shows himself out. Kristen continues to just stand there in the kitchen, overwhelmed with her feelings for Joseph. Kristen can only think of spending the rest of her life with him and she gets some butterflies in her stomach wondering if Joseph feels the same towards her.

Silent Knight

It is a warm and clear night in the city. It is an important night for the class of 1991. The bad weather kept postponing their prom so the class voted to have it on the night before graduation.

The gym is beautifully decorated. Students are everywhere, sitting, getting drinks, getting pictures and dancing to the live band. Joseph and Kristen are next in line for their prom pictures. Kristen can't believe how handsome Joseph looks in a tuxedo with tails. Joseph can't believe how beautiful Kristen looks in her emerald green dress that hugs her every curve and he can't believe she is wearing the bear claw necklace on such a formal night. As Joseph looks at Kristen, he knows that it was only natural for him to ask Kristen to the prom and he was so happy when she said yes. The couple in front of them step away from the camera and the two of them step in front of the camera for their pictures. Once the pictures are done, the next song starts. It is a slow love song.

Kristen and Joseph walk out on the dance floor and slowly start moving together. She puts her arms around his neck and Joseph puts his hands on Kristen's waist. They just look into each other's eyes and slowly move back and forth for the entire song. Once the song is over, Joseph goes to get some punch for Kristen and himself. His friend, Shawn, a senior that stands around 5'10" tall and weighs about 175 pounds with brown hair and brown eyes and wearing a black tuxedo, is by the punch bowl. Kristen is standing over by Shawn's date, a petite blond in a beautiful blue dress. Another slow love song starts.

Shawn looks over at the girls, "They look beautiful tonight."

Joseph smiles and looks over, "Man, they always look beautiful." He looks back to Shawn, "They just look more beautiful tonight."

Kristen looks over at Joseph the same time he looks back at her and they just smile at each other. The feelings just rush over him. He can't believe how blind he has been.

Shawn taps Joseph on the shoulder, "Hey, you okay Joe?"

Joseph blinks a couple of times and looks back to Shawn, "I'm okay. It's just, well, I'm in love with Kristen."

Shawn lets out a nice laugh and grabs his two cups of punch, "Tell me something the whole school doesn't already know."

Joseph grabs his two cups of punch and the two boys walk back over to their dates. Joseph hands Kristen her cup of punch and wonders if she feels the same about him. The four of them finish their punch and the next song starts.

Kristen smiles as she hears one of her favorite songs and she grabs Joseph's hand. They walk out onto the dance floor. It quickly becomes guys on one side and girls on the other. Both lines are dancing in unison. Each couple takes a turn dancing between the rows of boys and girls. Shawn and his date take their turn, then Joseph and Kristen take their turn. The dancing continues like that until the song ends and the next song begins. It is an upbeat rock and roll song. Joseph and Kristen stay on the dance floor and dance away to the rock and roll song.

Once the song is over, Kristen takes Joseph's hand, "How about some more punch?"

Joseph nods, "I'll go get it."

Joseph and Shawn goes to get more punch while Kristen and Shawn's date sit at a table as a more light-hearted love song starts.

Shawn speaks to Joseph while they wait, "So, have you told Kristen how you feel?"

Joseph looks over at Kristen and their eyes meet and their hearts connect. Right then they both know what the other is thinking and feeling. Neither can believe how obvious it was. Joseph and Kristen smile at each other.

Joseph looks back at Shawn, "I think she knows. Excuse me."

Joseph grabs the punch and heads for the table. Shawn grabs his punch and follows Joseph. As the four of them finish their punch, the DJ announces the last dance and plays Elvis Presley's song, Can't Help Falling In Love With You. Joseph takes Kristen's hand and they walk out onto the dance floor as the song starts.

Kristen places her head on Joseph's right shoulder and wraps her arms around his waist. Joseph puts his right hand on her lower back and his left hand gently runs through her hair.

About a minute into the song, Joseph whispers to Kristen, "I love you Kristen. I love you with all my heart."

Kristen leans back and looks lovingly into Joseph's eyes, "I love you too. All I want is to be with you for the rest of my life."

Joseph returns the loving look and smiles, "I wouldn't have it any other way."

The moment becomes too much for both of them. Their lips meet. It is a good, long kiss. It is their first real kiss since they met all those years ago. They just let themselves get lost in the moment.

Chapter 5

DATE - July 29th, 1991
San Francisco, CA

It is a hot summer city night. The humidity is up and so is the temperature. Mr. and Mrs. Lee have gone away for the weekend. Joseph, wearing sweatpants and a t-shirt, walks into the kitchen, takes off his shirt and starts wiping the sweat off his face because he just finished his workout. Even though it is Friday night, he is still devoted to his martial arts. He thinks about all that he has mastered, however, he is still working on the pressure points and weapons training. He grabs a bottle of water from the refrigerator and waits for Kristen to arrive. He was so happy that his parents were okay with Kristen staying over. Joseph remembers prom night vividly and things have only gotten better since. Joseph starts wiping his body down when the doorbell rings. Joseph walks to the front door and opens it.

Joseph smiles when he sees the woman he loves. He is completely taken with Kristen who has grown into an incredibly beautiful 5'4" 120 pound young woman with medium length brown hair which is pulled back into a ponytail and gorgeous sky blue eyes.

Joseph just stares for a second at Kristen in her tank top and tight jean shorts, "Hi Kristen. Come on in."

Kristen walks in carrying a gym bag in her right hand. She is smiling because she likes to see Joseph with his shirt off. She loves Joseph's 5'8" 155 pound rock hard physique with his short brown hair and green eyes.

Kristen puts her gym bag down and takes a seat on the couch, "I brought over a couple of movies to watch."

Joseph nods, "Well, go ahead and make yourself at home. I'm going to shower and change."

Joseph walks over and hugs Kristen.

Kristen playfully pushes Joseph back, "Yuck, you're all sweaty." She smiles, "Go shower."

Joseph winks at her and walks off to shower. Kristen goes into the kitchen and makes popcorn. She puts in a romantic comedy and waits for Joseph. In a few minutes, Joseph comes walking in wearing jeans and a t-shirt. He sits down on the couch next to Kristen and puts his arm around her. Kristen starts the movie. They sit back and enjoy the movie and popcorn.

When the credits start to roll, Joseph sits forward, "I'll refill the drinks if you want to get the next movie ready."

Kristen stands up, "Okay."

Joseph goes to the kitchen as Kristen switches out the movie in the VCR. She sits back down on the couch and waits for her man. Joseph walks back in, places the drinks down on the coffee table and sits next to Kristen. Kristen starts the movie. About an hour into the second movie, they start making out and they miss the last twenty minutes of the movie.

Once the second movie is over, they take the pop-corn bowls into the kitchen. Joseph starts some water to wash the bowls and pan. Kristen grabs a towel to dry them with.

Joseph washes the first bowl, "Those were some good movies."

He hands the bowl to Kristen.

Kristen dries the bowl, "I thought they would be."

She puts the bowl up.

Joseph washes the second bowl, "Do you want to watch some TV after this?"

Kristen smiles, "Why don't you read me some poetry from your books. Besides, we got a little sidetracked watching that last movie."

Once the dishes are done, Joseph goes to his bedroom and gets his two favorite poetry books. He sits down on the couch. Kristen lays down on the couch with her head in Joseph's lap. He reads her poetry for a short while and they both start getting tired. Kristen stares up at Joseph, she has never wanted Joseph more than now.

Joseph puts down the second book, "Why don't you take my room and I'll sleep out here."

Kristen smiles, "Come tuck me in."

Joseph grabs her bag and they walk into his bedroom. Joseph puts her bag down at the end of the bed. As soon as he turns around, Kristen kisses him passionately. The kissing leads to kissing and touching. Kristen removes Joseph's shirt and kisses his chest. Joseph removes Kristen's top and sees the bear claw hanging around her neck. They smile at each other, climb into bed and allow themselves to get lost in the moment.

DATE - July 30th, 1991
San Francisco, CA

Joseph just lays in his bed, enjoying the sounds of the birds chirping. He finally opens his eyes and stretches. Joseph looks over at the clock next to the bed. It shows that it is 7:22 am. He rolls over as Kristen walks in. She is wearing pajama shorts, his t-shirt with the bear claw under it and she has her hair pulled back into a ponytail. They share a loving smile. Joseph lays on his back as Kristen climbs into bed and straddles him. She leans down and kisses him.

Joseph puts his hands on her thighs, "Are you okay with last night?"

Kristen gives him an are you kidding look, "It wouldn't have happened if I wasn't ready." She sighs and smiles, "Last night was wonderful."

Joseph nods slightly and smiles, "Yes it was."

Kristen kisses him again, then climbs out of bed, "Come on sleepy head. Breakfast is ready."

Kristen heads off to the kitchen. Joseph climbs out of bed and puts his sweatpants on. He heads off for the kitchen to have breakfast with the woman he loves.

DATE - August 12th, 1991
San Francisco, CA

In the pitch black of the hot summer night, a black sedan sits in an alley in a seedy part of the city. The usual hustle and bustle of the city echoes in the distance. Varges Martoni is sitting in the backseat of a black sedan with dark tinted windows. Daniel is in the passenger's seat and another one of Papa Martoni's men is sitting in the driver's seat. Varges rolls the dark tinted window down about halfway. A young man in his early twenties dressed in jeans, t-shirt and a jean jacket vest approaches the car with a black backpack full of an illegal substance. The young man glances up and down the alley, obviously nervous.

The man stops about five feet from the car, unable to see into the backseat, "Varges, you in there?"

Varges puts his 9mm pistol out the window. The young man's eyes widen as he realizes that Varges Martoni does not intend to pay for the substance he is carrying in his backpack. Before the young man can react, Varges rapidly pulls the trigger. Five shots later, the young man falls.

Varges puts his pistol away, "Dan, get the backpack and lets go."

Daniel chuckles, "Yes sir."

Daniel gets out and walks over to the young man's body.

Daniel pulls the backpack from the dead body and speaks coldheartedly, "I guess this wasn't your night."

DATE - September 7th, 1991

San Francisco, CA

Joseph, still in his workout clothes, is sitting at his kitchen table. He is holding a piece of paper in each hand. Joseph looks at the two acceptance letters, each one from a different college. He knows Kristen has already enrolled in San Francisco State College for accounting. He plans on majoring in computers. He has one letter for the local college and one from the University of North Carolina. Joseph knows that he has to make a decision soon because the cutoff date is getting closer. Joseph hears the doorbell.

Mr. Lee answers the door, "Hello Kristen, please come in. Joseph is in the kitchen."

Kristen, wearing her blue jeans and t-shirt, walks into the kitchen. Joseph smiles and stands up holding the letter from North Carolina in his right hand and the letter from the local college in his left.

Kristen walks over to him, "Are you okay?"

Joseph shrugs, "I guess."

Kristen kisses him, "I just want what is best for you." She smiles lovingly, "We can make it work either way."

Joseph smiles, "You are so wonderful."

The look in Kristen's sky blue eyes and the loving smile answers the elusive question he has been pondering all morning. Joseph crumples the paper from the University of North Carolina and tosses it in the trash.

Joseph smiles, "There is no way I would make it through work and school without you."

Kristen steps up and puts her arms around Joseph, "I love you."

As they hug each other tight, Joseph can feel the bear claw necklace through Kristen's shirt.

Joseph lets himself get lost in her arms, "I love you too."

DATE - January 18th, 1992

San Francisco, CA

Mr. Lee, wearing his traditional martial arts uniform, is standing by the wall in the 20 foot by 20 foot open room. Joseph, wearing his usual sweatpants and t-shirt, is standing on the mats that lay across the middle of the room. Mr. Lee watches as Joseph completes the last of the knife fighting techniques. Once the last technique is completed, Joseph takes a deep breath. He can't believe he just completed four straight hours of training. He demonstrated every technique he has learned for Mr. Lee. Joseph knows he did every technique just as he was trained.

Mr. Lee nods his approval, "Come and sit."

Mr. Lee walks over to the edge of the mat and sits cross-legged. Joseph sits across from his adoptive father. Mr. Lee poses many questions and ideals about philosophy and life to Joseph over the next hour. Joseph answers with what is in his heart and soul. He holds nothing back and allows his mind to stay open. Mr. Lee's face shows no emotion the entire time, but on the inside, he can feel the pride swelling. Mr. Lee knows that Joseph's training has been a success. When the hour is finally over, Mr. Lee stands.

Mr. Lee bows to Joseph, "Your training is complete. There is nothing more I can teach you. Experience will be your teacher now."

Joseph stands and bows. He is speechless. He can't believe that he is finally done after all these years.

Mr. Lee smiles and places his right hand on Joseph's shoulder, "Use your training wisely my son."

Joseph smiles in return, "I will father."

Mr. Lee turns and walks out of the room. He continues to smile at the last words Joseph spoke to him. It was the first time Joseph has ever called him father. The pride finally overtakes Mr. Lee and a single tear rolls down his cheek.

Joseph goes to his bedroom to call Kristen and tell her what happened. Joseph sits on his bed and a tear comes to his eye as he thinks about the word, son. It was the first time Mr. Lee ever called him his son and it makes Joseph feel so proud.

DATE - April 1st, 1992
San Francisco, CA

It is an absolutely perfect spring day in the big city. Varges is standing in the middle of a large, empty warehouse near

Fisherman's Wharf. He can smell the water in the air as he awaits the sellers. Two of Papa Martoni's men flank Varges. The man on the right is carrying a briefcase. Two oriental men dressed in suits walk up to Varges and stop a few feet in front of him. Both oriental men stand about 5'8" tall. One man is in his twenties and the other looks to be in his fifties.

Varges nods at the older oriental man, "Mr. Nguyen, so glad you could make it. Do you have our package?"

Mr. Nguyen motions to the young man next to him, "Do you have the money?"

Varges shakes his head and replies rather seriously, "No." He pauses for a second and smiles, "April Fools."

Mr. Nguyen lets out an unenthusiastic laugh, "I don't have much of a sense of humor Varges."

Varges replies playfully, "You should learn to lighten up Mr. Nguyen. Being too serious will lead you to an early grave."

Mr. Nguyen goes to respond, but before he can, the young oriental man is hit in the chest by a high powered rifle and is blown off his feet. Mr. Nguyen is caught completely off guard as Varges pulls out his 9mm pistol and fires three shots. Mr. Nguyen falls next to the young man.

Varges walks over to the young oriental man and picks up the briefcase.

Varges looks over to Mr. Nguyen's body, "I told you being too serious would put you in an early grave."

Daniel makes his way down from the rafters and meets Varges and the others at their car.

Varges smiles at Daniel as he walks up, "Nice shooting Dan."

Daniel places his rifle bag in the open trunk of the car, "I do my best."

The two young men let out a nice laugh and climb into the backseat of the car. One of the other men closes the trunk and gets in the passenger's seat. The car drives off into the city streets.

DATE - August 6th, 1992
San Francisco, CA

It is a bright and sunny summer morning as a warm breeze blows across the water carrying a salt water smell to Half Moon Bay State Beach. Joseph parks his car a few blocks from the beach. Joseph and Kristen get out of the car. Joseph is wearing his swim trunks and a muscle shirt with flip flops. Kristen is wearing cutoff jean shorts and a sleeveless t-shirt with flip flops and has her hair pulled back into a ponytail to show off her beautiful sky blue eyes. Joseph grabs the ice chest out of the trunk and Kristen grabs the towels, beach ball and Frisbee out of the backseat. It is only a little past 8 am, but they wanted to get to the beach before it started to get crowded.

Joseph and Kristen walk along the beach for about a hundred yards. The two of them stop and Kristen puts down the things she is carrying and sets up the towels as Joseph puts down the ice chest. They go for a walk along the beach since there is only a few other people there right now. They just hold hands and enjoy a nice, quiet walk together. About twenty minutes later, they return to the towels. A few other people have started to show up. They sit down on their towels and Joseph opens the ice chest.

Joseph grabs an apple, "I'm so glad we got the chance to do this. Even with taking fewer credit hours, between college and work, I felt like I didn't even have time to breath."

Kristen grabs a banana and closes the ice chest, "I know, college was so busy."

They eat their fruit and share work and college stories. A little over an hour later, Kristen stands up and takes off her t-shirt and jean shorts to reveal her incredible body in her two piece bathing suit and the bear claw necklace hanging around her neck. Joseph removes his shirt to expose his muscular physique. Then the two of them grab the beach ball and Frisbee and head for the water. Kristen just stares at Joseph's nice physique. Joseph can't take his eyes off Kristen and her two piece bathing suit. The beach starts to get busy now. They play around in the water for awhile, throwing the Frisbee and beach ball around. It starts getting closer to noon so they get out of the water and head for their towels. The two of them dry off and sit down. Joseph grabs his watch and sees it is about 11:45 am.

Joseph looks at Kristen, "Are you hungry?"

Kristen nods, "Yea, kind of."

The two of them make some sandwiches and eat. The talking dies down, giving way to kissing. After the few minutes of kissing stops, they see a guys on girls volleyball game going on.

Kristen smiles at Joseph, "So, do you want to try your luck."

Joseph returns the smile, "You may kick my butt at basketball, but I'll get even with volleyball."

Kristen replies sarcastically, "Well, bring it on."

Joseph and Kristen join in and play volleyball for a couple of hours. After a few games of volleyball they head back to the water to swim some more.

Kristen wades in up to her knees, then splashes water up at Joseph, "Get even huh?"

Joseph just smiles, "Okay, so volleyball is not my game either." He pause, then a devilish look crosses his face, "But I do know what I'm good at."

Kristen can tell by his look that Joseph has something planned, "Don't even think about whatever it is your thinking about."

Joseph quickly moves close to Kristen and sweeps her up off her feet into his arms.

Joseph jokes with her, "I'm kind of tired, I don't know if I can hold you."

Kristen's eyes widen, "Don't even think about dunking me in the water."

Joseph just smiles, "Thought about it."

Joseph drops Kristen into the water. Her whole body and head goes under the water. Kristen pops up out of the water and gets back on her feet to hear Joseph laughing.

Kristen quickly checks to ensure the necklace is still on, then fixes her ponytail, "Oh, you are so going to get it now."

Joseph just continues to laugh. He looks at his watch and sees it is about 4:30 pm now. The beach is starting to clear out some. The two of them get out of the water and head back to their towels. They dry off and eat some more fruit and another sandwich. Once done eating, Joseph takes the ice chest back to the car. Kristen watches him walk off. She is wanting him really bad now.

Joseph gets back to the beach to see Kristen standing under one of the beach showers. Seeing Kristen in her bathing suit under the shower is making Joseph really want her. He walks up and gives her a hug and a kiss.

Kristen leans back from Joseph, "I see, now you want to love up on me."

Joseph pulls her close and they share a nice kiss. They each wash off and head back to their towels.

Kristen sits down, "How can you be so wonderful?"

Joseph is surprised by the question and can only think of one response, "It's easy when it comes to you."

Kristen smiles and stares into Joseph's eyes, "You've always been there for me. I can just feel the love in your arms and see it in your eyes."

Joseph just smiles back and returns the passionate stare, "I love you more than anything else, and I can just feel your love for me."

Kristen moves against Joseph, "There's something more. You just have a certain way with me."

Joseph can see it in Kristen's eyes. He feels the same way. With the beach now empty around them, it is the perfect moment. Kristen lays back on her towel. Joseph moves to her covering them with his towel and they just let the moment lead them.

DATE - April 12th, 1993
San Francisco, CA

It is a nice spring evening as the sun has started to get lower in the sky. Joseph, who is wearing Dockers and a collared shirt, finishes lighting the candles on the dinner table. He was so happy when his parents went away for the weekend giving him a chance to have a nice dinner with Kristen. He hears the doorbell ring. He turns off the last light in the house and heads for the door.

Joseph opens the door and smiles, "Hello Kristen, come in."

Kristen walks in and they hug and kiss. She is wearing a nice, form fitting spring dress with her hair pulled back into a ponytail. Kristen notices all the lights are off and a soft glow coming from the dining room.

Kristen smiles, "What's going on?"

Joseph doesn't say a word, he just puts his right hand on Kristen's lower back and leads her to the dining room. Kristen sees the spaghetti and garlic bread waiting. Joseph pulls out her chair and Kristen sits. He fixes her a plate and pours her some ice tea. Kristen just watches Joseph. Joseph fixes him a plate and pours himself some ice tea. He turns on some soft music and returns to the table. Joseph sits across from Kristen. As they eat, the conversation begins.

Kristen smiles, "This is quite a surprise. I was wondering why you asked me to wear a dress."

Joseph puts down his glass, "I just thought it would be nice since we haven't had a special date in awhile."

Kristen sits back, "I know, things have been so busy lately."

Joseph nods in agreement, "Amen to that."

They just stare at each other for a minute, each thinking the same thing. Once they finish eating, Joseph gets up and walks over to Kristen.

Joseph holds out his hand, "May I have this dance."

Kristen takes his hand, "I would be delighted."

They walk into the living room and slow dance for a couple of songs. They kiss occasionally. On the third song, the kissing gets a little more passionate.

Kristen stares into Joseph's eyes, "Lets go to your room."

Joseph picks Kristen up and carries her to his room. He lays her down in his bed and lays down next to her. The passion continues and once they are finished making love, Kristen drifts off to sleep in Joseph's arms.

Joseph lays awake thinking about how much he loves Kristen and all the wonderful times they have had together. He watches her sleep. The glow on her face, her quiet breathing, he is totally taken with her. He kisses her forehead, touches the bear claw that hangs around her neck and holds her tight. In an hour, he drifts off to sleep, thankful to be sharing his life with Kristen.

DATE - September 20th, 1993
San Francisco, CA

Papa Martoni is sitting in his den, enjoying the morning paper. Varges walks in and sits across from his father.

Papa Martoni speaks without looking away from his paper, "How did collection go?"

Varges shrugs, "Not bad Papa. Mr. Wilson has refused to pay again."

Papa Martoni lowers his paper, "That is two months in a row."

Varges nods hoping to hear his father give him the go ahead to take care of the situation, "Yes it is. What do you want me to do about it?"

Papa Martoni is quiet for a few seconds, "I think it's time to send another message to everyone." He pauses, "Make sure it is taken care of."

Varges smiles hearing exactly what he wanted to from his father, "Yes sir."

Varges gets up and walks out as Papa Martoni returns to reading his paper.

Chapter 6

DATE - June 1st, 1994
San Francisco, CA

Joseph walks into his bedroom with a towel wrapped around his waist. He just finished a shower after his evening workout. He changes into a pair of gym shorts and a loose fitting t-shirt. He walks over to his radio and turns it on. He puts it on a country music station when he hears the front doorbell ring. Joseph knows that his mom and dad are probably in the garden so he puts on his house shoes and heads for the front door.

As Joseph approaches the front door, the doorbell rings again, "Just a minute!"

Joseph opens the door to see Kristen standing there in her jean shorts and tank top. He smiles at first, but then realizes the tears running down her cheeks.

Joseph questions, "Kristen, what's wrong?"

Kristen runs into Joseph's arms. She squeezes him so tight that he can feel the bear claw through her top and he reassuringly hugs her back.

Joseph questions again, "Kristen, what is it?"

Kristen manages a few words, "Bobby Kerns. He said some ..." She sniffles, "Some very bad things."

Joseph speaks caringly, "Come in and have a seat."

The two of them walk into the living room and sit on the couch.

Joseph continues to hold Kristen, "What did Bobby say?"

Kristen is a little unsure, knowing how it is going to affect Joseph, "I'm not sure, I'm ..."

Kristen stops and looks down.

Joseph lifts her chin up with his left hand, "Kristen, you can tell me."

Kristen sniffles again. Finally, Kristen tells Joseph about the hurtful rumors Bobby spread about her. She then explains how she confronted Bobby about the rumors and how he verbally abused her. Joseph sits and listens intently and with each passing word, his temperature rises.

When Kristen finishes, Joseph hugs her close, "Look, I'll go and talk to Bobby."

Kristen looks up at Joseph, "Bobby is crazy, you know about him. I don't want you to get in trouble or get hurt."

Joseph gives a reassuring smile, "I'm just going to talk to him, that's all. It's going to be okay, I'll take care of it. Okay?"

Kristen nods slightly and falls back into Joseph's arms. Joseph hugs her tight. All he can think about is dealing with Bobby Kerns.

DATE - June 14th, 1994
San Francisco, CA

It is a warm, but overcast summer day as Joseph and Kristen pull up in front of the downtown Tae Kwon Do school. Joseph remembers vividly how this moment arrived. A couple of weeks ago, Kristen came to his house crying. A guy that use to like Kristen, Bobby Kerns, spread some rumors about her that were untrue. When Kristen said something to Bobby about it, he verbally abused her until she cried. Joseph remembers opening the door and seeing Kristen standing there in tears. Joseph confronted Bobby and demanded an apology. Bobby refused and told Joseph the only way he would apologize would be to have it beaten out of him. Today, Joseph plans on doing just that. Joseph knows that Bobby is really good, but he doesn't think he should have any problems with him. Joseph, wearing some baggy shorts and t-shirt, and Kristen, wearing jean shorts and a t-shirt, get out of the car. Joseph grabs his gym bag from the backseat and the two of them walk into the dojo. All of the students are standing around the 50 foot by 50 foot mat. Bobby, a stout young man that stands about 5'11" tall and weighs near 195 pounds dressed in a traditional martial arts uniform, and his instructor are standing in the middle of the mat waiting.

Kristen looks at Joseph with concern, "You don't have to do this Joseph."

Joseph slightly shakes his head, "It's too late to turn back now."

Kristen looks down, "I don't want to see you get hurt."

Joseph raises her chin and places his hand on the bear claw necklace that hangs under her shirt, "I'll be fine."

Kristen remembers what Joseph told her about the necklace and something in his smile makes her feel better. Joseph goes into the back and changes into his sweatpants and t-shirt. A couple minutes later, he is standing in the middle of the mat with Bobby and his instructor.

The instructor speaks, "Anything goes and it's not over until someone quits or gets knocked out."

Bobby and Joseph nod at the same time. The instructor walks over next to Kristen as Bobby and Joseph take their fighting stances. This would be the first time Kristen has ever seen Joseph in action.

The instructor issues his command, "Begin!"

Bobby throws a kick at Joseph's lead leg, but Joseph steps back and the kick misses. Bobby throws a straight right punch at Joseph's head. Joseph slaps it away with his lead hand as he moves right. Bobby feints with his left leg and throws a roundhouse kick with his right leg at Joseph's head. Joseph ducks under the kick and steps back. Bobby comes back around to his stance.

Bobby speaks frustrated, "Come on chicken, fight!"

Joseph smiles at Bobby's frustration, knowing he has Bobby right where he wants him now. Joseph moves around for a few seconds. Bobby doesn't realize what Joseph is doing, then, like a flash of lightning, Joseph's lead hand snaps out and smashes into Bobby's nose. Bobby's head snaps back, his knees go a little weak and the blood begins to run instantly. Bobby shakes his head and looks at Joseph in surprise. Joseph can see the fear in Bobby's eyes now. A couple seconds later, Joseph's lead hand smashes into Bobby's nose again. Right after that, Joseph sweeps Bobby's feet and Bobby falls to the ground. Joseph shuffles back and Bobby quickly scrambles to his feet.

Joseph steps in and feints a punch. Bobby throws up his right hand to block. Joseph grabs the back of Bobby's right wrist and twists it. The pain causes Bobby to bend forward and when he does, Joseph knees him in the face. Bobby's knees go weak. Joseph kicks his leg over Bobby's arm to where he is straddling the arm with his back to Bobby. Joseph then rolls forward and before Bobby realizes it, he is on his back in a straight arm bar. Bobby struggles for a few seconds and then starts to feel the cartilage in his elbow and shoulder start to give. Bobby taps Joseph on the arm a couple of times to signify that he gives up. Joseph lets go and quickly gets back on his feet. Kristen runs over and throws her arms around him.

Kristen kisses Joseph, "I love you so much. I'm so happy you're okay."

Joseph smiles, "I'm fine. There's just one more thing."

Kristen steps back. Joseph stands next to Bobby as Bobby gets to his knees. Joseph grabs one of the pressure points in Bobby's neck. Bobby winces in pain.

Joseph grips a little harder, "I believe you have something to say."

Bobby looks up at Kristen, "I'm sorry. I didn't mean all those things I said."

Kristen smiles proudly, "Let him go Joseph. He's not worth any more of our time."

Joseph releases Bobby, "Don't ever speak of or to Kristen again, because from here, it only gets worse."

Joseph retrieves his bag and he and Kristen walk out. Kristen takes hold of Joseph's hand and she can't stop smiling. She is so proud that her man defended her honor and she also is surprised at how good Joseph really is.

DATE - July 20th, 1994
San Francisco, CA

The sun is shining on an incredibly beautiful summer day. The sounds of the city echo in the background. Joseph, wearing sandals, jean shorts and a t-shirt, pulls up in front of Kristen's house. Kristen comes running out wearing her usual t-shirt, jean shorts and sandals and she is carrying a picnic basket. She puts the basket in the back seat next to a blanket and climbs in the passenger's seat next to Joseph. They give each other a kiss and Joseph drives off.

Kristen smiles as the wind blows through her hair, "So, where are you taking me again?"

Joseph shakes his head and smiles, "I promised to take you to my special place. So that is where we are going."

They drive for about thirty minutes and finally arrive at a secluded place near the bay. It is a large open plot of plush green grass, with some trees and a few bushes and a view of the bay in the distance. Kristen is awestruck by the amazing view. Joseph parks the car and the two of them get out. Joseph grabs the ice chest from the trunk and Kristen grabs the blanket and the basket. She sets down the basket and places the blanket about 75 feet from the bay. Joseph puts down the ice chest.

Kristen looks out over the bay, "It's so beautiful here. I've lived in this city my whole life, but I've never been here before."

Joseph smiles, "I found it when I went out running one day. It is beautiful," He looks over at Kristen, "Even more so with you here."

Kristen looks at Joseph and smiles, "Thank you."

She kisses him and they sit down to have lunch. After lunch, they go for a walk. They talk, laugh and hold hands. It's a nice slow walk and about an hour later, they arrive back at their picnic spot.

Joseph kisses Kristen, "I have a surprise for you."

Kristen looks at him closely, "What is it?"

Joseph smiles, "Wait here, and close your eyes."

Kristen chuckles and closes her eyes, "You better not scare me."

Joseph walks over to his car, "No way. I value my life too much."

Kristen chuckles and shakes her head. Joseph opens the trunk and pulls out a fishing pole and tackle box. He walks back over to Kristen.

Joseph speaks, "You can open your eyes now."

Kristen opens her eyes in surprise, "A fishing pole."

Joseph nods, "You told me that you've never been fishing before and I said I would take you some day."

Kristen grabs the pole excitedly, "Lets go."

The two of them walk down to the bank of the bay. Joseph puts down the tackle box and pulls out the bait.

Kristen looks at the bait and loses her smile, "Worms."

Joseph chuckles at her reaction, "Let me see the pole."

Joseph bait's the hook. He shows Kristen how to cast. Kristen gives it a few tries, almost throwing the pole in the water the first time and nearly hitting Joseph once. She can't keep from laughing. Joseph laughs with her. After quite a few tries, Kristen gets a good cast. Joseph explains fishing to Kristen. They sit, talk and fish for about an hour. Suddenly the pole jerks and Kristen screams quickly.

Joseph quickly speaks, "Okay, you need to pull back on the pole until it is straight up in the air and then turn the reel until the pole is flat down again."

Kristen tugs and reels, not sure of what she is doing. Joseph tries not to laugh as he continues to explain to Kristen what to do. She finally gets in the rhythm and Kristen manages to reel in her first fish.

Kristen looks at the fish hanging from the end of the pole, "Look at it. It's so beautiful." She looks over at Joseph, "We can't let it die."

Joseph looks at her, "What?"

Kristen gets a look of concern, "Please Joseph, I don't want to see the fish die."

Joseph just smiles at Kristen, amazed at how much she just, loves. Joseph takes the pole and gets the fish off the hook. Joseph throws the fish back into the water. Joseph gathers up the fishing items and returns them to the car as Kristen prepares dinner.

As they eat, Kristen speaks, "That was so much fun. Thanks Joseph."

Joseph smiles, "I told you it's fun."

Kristen puts down her bottle of water, "I love you so much."

Joseph finishes his last bite of dinner, "I do these things because I love you."

Once Kristen finishes her dinner, Joseph takes the basket back to the car. Kristen watches him walk back. She has made up her mind.

Joseph sits next to Kristen, "We have a couple more hours. Is there anything else you would like to do or anywhere you want to go?"

Kristen puts her arms around Joseph and stares into his eyes, "I have everything I want right here."

Kristen kisses him passionately. She lays back and Joseph moves to her. As Joseph lifts her shirt up, he sees the bear claw around her neck. Joseph and Kristen smile at each other. They continue to kiss and touch as they lose themselves in the moment.

DATE - October 31st, 1994
San Francisco, CA

As the darkness of Halloween falls across the city, the city comes alive with parties to celebrate the holiday. The Martoni home is no different. The huge mansion is decorated in a festive Halloween mood. The home is packed with family and friends enjoying the Halloween party.

Varges and Daniel, both still dressed in their business suits, walk in the front door.

They walk up to one of Papa Martoni's men and Varges questions, "Where is Papa?"

The man replies cheerfully, "Happy Halloween boss. He's in the den."

Varges and Daniel walk off to the den. They see Papa Martoni standing with a small group of people and start making their way to him. Varges and Daniel greet various friends and family as they make their way through the crowd.

Varges stops next to his father and speaks only loud enough for Papa Martoni to hear him, "It's done. No more witnesses."

Papa Martoni nods and quietly replies, "And the detective?"

Daniel reassures Papa Martoni, "He has nothing, but we still have our eye on him."

Papa Martoni smiles, "Good. Enough work for today. You boys go and enjoy the party now."

Varges and Daniel each give Papa Martoni a hug and walk off to mingle with some of their friends.

DATE - February 14th, 1995
San Francisco, CA

The sun has set in the city as Kristen looks at herself in her bedroom mirror. She smiles at what she sees. She plans on knocking Joseph's socks off with her tight jeans and t-shirt. She didn't tell him that he would be the only one coming over for her birthday or that her parents are gone for a few days. The doorbell rings and she goes to answer it.

Kristen opens the door, "Hey Joseph, come in."

Joseph, wearing blue jeans and a t-shirt, is speechless when he sees Kristen in her tight clothes. Joseph likes it when Kristen wears clothes that shows off her incredible body because she doesn't wear those kind of clothes that often. Joseph is holding a present in his left hand.

Joseph walks in and puts the present on the coffee table, "Are we the only one's here?"

Kristen smiles, walks over to the radio and starts some music, "I wanted us to have a special night together."

She takes his hand and they dance to a slow song. They kiss some while dancing. Once the song is finished, the two of them sit on the couch. Kristen grabs the present.

Joseph looks at her, "Whoa, what are you doing? You can't open presents without cake and ice cream first."

Kristen gives him a sly smile, "Don't worry, you'll get desert later, but it won't be cake and ice cream."

Joseph gives her an exciting smile, "I like the sound of that."

Kristen opens the present. She throws her arms around Joseph and kisses him.

Joseph smiles, "I take it you like the gift."

Kristen playfully pushes his shoulder, "I love it."

She opens her new CD and puts it in the stereo. She takes Joseph's hand and they dance to the new slow song that Kristen loves so much.

Once the song is over, Kristen looks into Joseph's eyes, "Thank you for the poetry books."

Joseph smiles, "I know how much you like them. Besides, I think I know every poem by heart."

Kristen doesn't quite know what to say next, then the only logical thing comes out, "I love you Joseph."

Kristen starts to say something else, but Joseph puts his right index finger up to her lips. He knows what she was going to say from the look in her eyes. Joseph picks her up and carries Kristen off to her room. He puts her down at the end of the bed. They start kissing and touching. Soon they are under the covers and Joseph is laying on Kristen.

Joseph glances at the bear claw around Kristen's neck, then places his left hand on Kristen's cheek, "I love you Kristen, with all that I am."

They kiss and let the moment take them. Once the loving is over, they lay in each other's arms.

Kristen speaks softly, "What do you think the future will bring?"

Joseph is quiet for a few seconds and replies softly, "I see happy times, loving times." He pauses, "With you."

Kristen smiles and kisses Joseph, "Me too."

They lay quietly for a little longer, then Joseph drifts off to sleep. Kristen watches him sleep. She loves it when they make love. She loves feeling their bodies laying together. Kristen watches Joseph for a few more minutes and then drifts off to dream.

DATE - June 30th, 1995
San Francisco, CA

It is a warm, clear morning in the big city. Varges and Daniel are sitting in a booth and enjoying a morning cup of coffee at a local coffee shop. Detective Jackson walks up and tosses a picture of two dead bodies on the table.

Varges looks up and smiles, "Detective Jackson, what a pleasant surprise." He motions to the seat next to Daniel, "Would you care to join us?"

Detective Jackson taps the picture, "I don't suppose you recognize these men?"

Varges glances his eyes at the picture, "Sorry. Don't think I know them."

Detective Jackson looks over at Daniel, "How about you?"

Daniel smiles, "Sorry detective."

Detective Jackson sighs, "They were shot ten times, but you wouldn't know anything about that."

Varges gives a sarcastic smile, "Sorry, but I'm just a businessman. Wish I could help, but you know how it is."

Detective Jackson snatches up the picture, "Just wanted to let you know that I'm still around and that I'm watching."

Varges nods, "You have a good day detective."

Detective Jackson walks out, hoping he made an impact.

Varges looks at Daniel, "I almost feel sorry for him. He really believes in what he's doing." Varges pauses and gives an evil smile, "Almost."

Daniel motions for the check. The waitress brings the check over. Daniel tosses the money on the table and the two men walk out of the coffee shop.

DATE - July 5th, 1996
California

The sun is starting to set over the open California land. Kristen, wearing her tight fitting jean shorts and tank top, smiles as the breeze blows through her hair. Joseph, wearing jean shorts and a t-shirt, has the top down on the GTO. The two of them are headed to Mexico for a vacation and they are traveling south on Interstate 5 right now. Joseph takes the car up to 80 mph. The road is wide open and they haven't seen very many vehicles on the road.

Kristen screams in enjoyment, "This is awesome!"

Joseph smiles at Kristen. Kristen turns up the hard rock song on the radio, puts her hair back into a ponytail, puts the bear claw necklace inside her tank top and stands up in the front seat, holding onto the top of the windshield with her left hand for support. She holds up her right hand and extends the index and pinky finger. She starts rocking her hand and her head back and forth with the music. Joseph glances over Kristen's sexy body in her tight clothes and shakes his head.

When the song ends, Kristen sits back down, "I love this car!"

They go for another hour until Joseph stops for gas. Once the tank is full and drinks purchased, they hit the highway again. Kristen plays with the radio until she finds the right song. She leans over and Joseph puts his arm around her. Kristen kisses him on the cheek, then slides her hand down below his waist.

Joseph sits up in his seat, quite surprised, "Kristen?"

Kristen whispers in his ear, "Relax, I won't hurt you."

Joseph does his best to concentrate on the road, but he doesn't remember much of the highway for the next few miles. All he can think about is Kristen, the music and the memories.

DATE - July 6th, 1996
San Francisco, CA

Papa Martoni has just finished his dinner and he now sits in his chair in the den. Two of his men are sitting on the couch across from him. One man is wearing a blue suit and looks to be in his forties. The other man is in a gray suit and appears to be in his late twenties.

The older man speaks, "It's finally done. We got rid of the last of the competition today."

Papa Martoni breathes a sigh of relief, but he has an uneasy look on his face, "Good. At least for now, we can stop the bloodshed."

The younger man speaks, "What about the locals?"

Papa Martoni motions with his hand, "They are small time, not worth our effort. We just need to make sure no one tries to move in."

Papa Martoni winces as he feels sharp pain his chest and he starts to lose feeling in his left arm.

The older man can tell something is wrong, "Boss, are you okay?"

Papa Martoni tries to take a breath, but finds it is hard to come by. He tries to say something, but he ends up slumping over and falling to the floor.

The older man rushes to Papa Martoni as the younger man runs to the phone and calls 911. The ambulance arrives shortly after the phone call. The older man gets in the ambulance with Papa Martoni. The younger man calls Varges to tell him what is going on as the ambulance speeds away.

Varges and Daniel arrive at the hospital about an hour later. They walk down the hallway and they see the older man that rode with Papa Martoni standing outside a hospital room door.

Varges walks up to the older man, "How is he?"

The older man sighs, "He's okay now."

Varges questions, "What happened?"

The older man replies, "Your father had a heart attack."

Varges looks at the floor and shakes his head, not wanting to believe what he just heard. Daniel puts his left hand on Varges' right shoulder for support.

The older man speaks reassuringly, "He's awake and he's been waiting on you."

Varges puts his left hand on the older man's shoulder, "Thanks Tony."

Tony gives Varges a slight nod. Varges walks into the room to check on his father and Tony and Daniel take a seat outside the room.

DATE - July 8th, 1996
San Francisco, CA

Detective Jackson has been sitting at his desk for the better part of the afternoon. He sits back in his chair and tosses the folder in his hand onto the desk, on top of numerous other folders. He can't accept the fact that Papa Martoni walked free and that he has no evidence to go after Varges Martoni.

A female detective walks up, "Jackson, have you heard the news?"

Detective Jackson looks up, "What news?"

The detective smiles, "Papa Martoni had a heart attack the other day. He left the hospital this morning."

Detective Jackson sits forward and grabs another folder, "Maybe his heart will do what I failed at."

The detective pats him on the shoulder, "Don't beat yourself up over one lost case."

The detective walks off. Detective Jackson knows he has taken the case personally. He has been after the Martoni family since he first became a detective. He also thinks about his father's murder case. His father was gunned down in the street and nothing ever happened to the shooter. Worst of all, he tried reopening his father's case and was unable to close it.

Detective Jackson opens the file and speaks to himself, "There has to be something I'm missing. Something to bring down the Martoni family."

DATE - July 10th, 1996

Mexico

It is a warm, dry and overcast day in the Mexican village. Joseph, wearing jean shorts, a t-shirt and sandals, and Kristen, wearing jean shorts, a tank top and sandals, walk from shop to shop looking at all the gifts and wondering what they should get for their parents. Kristen is also looking for a nice dress for the fiesta tonight.

They stop at a jewelry shop and Joseph picks up a turquoise necklace, "I think your mom would really like this."

Kristen looks at the necklace, "Wow, that's beautiful." She pulls out the bear claw necklace from under her shirt, "Not as nice as mine, but your right, she would love that."

Joseph leans over and kisses Kristen's cheek, "I love you."

They shop for a couple more hours before returning to their room with their gifts. They lay around for the next few hours as darker clouds start to move in. Once the sun starts to set, the two of them change into the Mexican clothes that they bought for the fiesta and head for the town square and the fiesta. The temperature has dropped some and the smell of rain is in the air. Not caring about the changing weather, Joseph and Kristen dance, drink and party for an hour. A few raindrops start to fall. It is a light rain for about ten minutes, then the rain starts to fall a little harder. Everyone moves under the canopies covering the fronts of the local shops. Everyone stands around waiting to see if the rain is going to stop.

Joseph looks at the older Mexican man standing next to him, "Is this usual for this time of year?"

The man replies in broken English, "No, it is usually nice. It would be too bad if we could not continue. This is our yearly fiesta to celebrate love."

Kristen takes hold of Joseph's hand, "I can't wait any longer. It's just rain. Come on, lets dance."

Joseph just smiles as Kristen leads him back out into the square. They start slow dancing even though there is no music. The band is inspired by the two Americans and not a minute later, the band starts playing again and everyone else starts back into the square. The fiesta goes on, but after another hour, Joseph and Kristen make their way back to their room. Still soaking wet from the rain, they slow dance in their room to the music in the background.

Joseph looks into Kristen's eyes, "I love you so much."

Kristen starts to undo the buttons on the front of her dress, "I love you too."

They start kissing and don't even bother drying off. Once again, they let themselves get lost in the magical moment.

DATE - August 14th, 1996
San Francisco, CA

It's an extremely hot, summer Saturday as Joseph, who is wearing baggy shorts, t-shirt and sandals, unlocks the door to the newly renovated studio apartment. Kristen is with him, and other than wearing the usual jean shorts, tank top, sandals and bear claw necklace, she is also wearing a blindfold.

They step inside and Joseph removes the blindfold, "Okay, what do you think?"

Kristen looks around at the apartment. The huge open room has hard wood floors, a couch, chair, entertainment center, coffee table and two end tables on the east side of the room. The west side of the room has some workout equipment, a bed and a walk-in closet. She can see the kitchen in the back and a door that leads to the bathroom and laundry room. The place is decorated in an oriental motif.

Kristen smiles, "I love it." She looks at Joseph, "Why are we here?"

Joseph smiles, "This is my new place. I moved in over the weekend."

Kristen looks around in amazement, "Why didn't you tell me?"

Joseph takes her hand, "I wanted to surprise you."

Joseph gives Kristen a tour of the place and once they are done walking around, they have a seat on the couch.

Kristen leans over against Joseph, "It's going to be so nice to have a place where we can be alone, without parents." She pauses, "But how can you afford this place?"

Joseph puts his arm around her, "I had a trust fund left to me from my birth parents. Since I got a scholarship, I didn't need the money for college. With my job that I've had for awhile, I only needed some of the money to help pay for my car and motorcycle. I did some math and found that I can afford this place, so I moved in."

Kristen smiles, "This is going to be so awesome and it's not that far from our boat."

DATE - September 1st, 1996
San Francisco, CA

William Shobe tosses his paper plate in the trash after he finishes his sandwiches he had for lunch. He opens the refrigerator and grabs a bottle of water. At that time, the phone rings.

William Shobe walks over and answers the phone, "Hello."

Joseph speaks, "Hello Mr. Shobe. Is Kristen there?"

William replies, "No she isn't. She is at our boat. I can take a message if you would like."

Joseph responds, "That's okay. I'm suppose to pick her up so we can enroll in our last year of college. I can just swing by the boat and pick her up."

William questions, "Do you know where the boat is at?"

Joseph sounds unsure, "I know it's next to Fisherman's Wharf, but I'm not sure of the pier or dock number."

William explains, "It is dock number 12, pier 4."

Joseph replies, "Thanks Mr. Shobe."

William smiles, "Okay. Take care Joe."

They hang up, Joseph changes into some jeans, long sleeve t-shirt and his boots, then grabs his two motorcycle helmets and goes down to the garage. He gets on his motorcycle. It is a blue and yellow high speed street bike. He usually only rides alone, but he has had it for a year now and he has never taken Kristen for a ride. Besides, it is a special occasion, their last college enrollment.

It doesn't take Joseph long to reach the docks. He pulls up by the gate that leads to dock 12. He sees Kristen, in her tight jeans and long sleeve t-shirt, walking towards the gate. Joseph takes off his helmet and waits for her.

Kristen walks up, "Awesome. I finally get to ride on your bike."

Joseph smiles, "Ready for our last enrollment."

Kristen nods happily, "Oh yea."

Joseph hands Kristen the second helmet. Kristen lets out her ponytail and tucks the bear claw necklace under her shirt. They put the helmets on and Joseph turns the bike around. Kristen climbs on the back and they head off for the college.

Chapter 7

DATE - May 12th, 1997
San Francisco, CA

Joseph and Kristen, wearing their caps and gowns, continue to sit patiently in the folding chairs in the middle of the gym at their college. The decorated gym is full of family and friends that came to see the class of 1997 receive their degrees. Mr. and Mrs. Lee are sitting next to William and Becky Shobe. The graduating class listens to the last speech from the dean of the college.

It seems like an eternity to all the students, but the dean of the college finishes his graduation speech, "So I say, go forth and do great things class of 1997. Good luck and God bless."

All the students stand up as the crowd of family and friends cheer. The caps fly as the graduates celebrate. Kristen and Joseph shakes hands, congratulate and hug all their friends as they make their way towards each other. They find each other in the crowd.

Joseph and Kristen speak at the same time, "Congratulations."

The two of them hug and kiss. Kristen's parents walk up followed by Mr. and Mrs. Lee.

William speaks, "Congratulations, both of you."

Becky smiles at the two kids, "I'm so proud of you both."

Kristen, who still has her arm around Joseph, smiles, "So, are we still going to dinner?"

Mr. Lee responds happily, "Of course, this is a day for celebration."

Joseph nods in agreement, "We should get going. It's going to take some time to get out of the parking lot."

Kristen looks at her mom and dad, "I'll ride to the restaurant with Joseph."

They all hug each other again and the six of them start making their way through the crowd. Joseph and Kristen both have the look of someone who can't wait to see what the future will bring now.

DATE - May 28th, 1997
San Francisco, CA

It's mid-evening and Kristen and Joseph are sitting on his couch in his apartment. Joseph is wearing jeans and a t-shirt. He wanted to keep the night casual as to not give away his intentions. Joseph plans on this being a special evening. Kristen is wearing her jean shorts and tank top with her hair pulled back into a ponytail. The two of them are just listening to music and looking through a scrapbook that Kristen made.

Kristen looks at Joseph, "What was the name of the song we fell in love to at the prom?"

Joseph smiles, "That's easy. It was Elvis Presley's, 'Can't Help Falling In Love With You'."

Kristen nods, "Good memory."

Joseph gives a knowing shrug, "I expect you to re-member the name of the song we get engaged to."

Kristen chuckles, "That's something I would never forget."

The conversation continues about old times and the different job interviews they each have had. The night is going just the way Joseph had hoped. Joseph waits about an hour, when he is sure Kristen has forgotten the en-gagement comment, when he gets up and puts a new CD in the CD player. He sets it to a certain song and pushes play. The song, Love Will Keep Us Alive, by the Eagles comes on.

Joseph sits next to Kristen and she looks at him, "You got the Eagles CD? What are all the songs on it?"

Joseph points at the stereo, "I can't remember all the songs, but the CD case is on the stereo."

Kristen puts down the scrapbook, gets up and walks over to the stereo. Although his nerves are starting to show, Joseph quietly walks up behind her. As Kristen picks up the CD case, Joseph pulls a quarter carat, heart shaped diamond ring out of his pocket with his slightly shaking hand. Kristen reads the back of the CD case as Joseph drops to his right knee, being ever so quiet.

As Kristen turns around, Joseph holds the ring up and speaks the words, "Kristen, will you marry me?"

Kristen's face is that of complete shock. She was not prepared for this at all. She wants to reply, but the words have trouble coming out. A couple tears roll down her cheek.

Finally, Kristen is able to give her answer, "Yes, God yes. I'll marry you."

Joseph smiles, slides the ring on her finger and stands up.

Joseph hugs her tight, "I love you Kristen, with all my heart. I'll always love you."

Kristen is still in shock and not able to say anything, but she squeezes Joseph so tight he can feel the bear claw under her top. The hug is all the reassurance Joseph needs.

DATE - June 8th, 1997
San Francisco, CA

Joseph, still in his sleeping clothes, is doing some morning cleaning in his apartment when he hears his phone ring.

Joseph walks over and answers his phone, "Hello."

Kristen speaks with her usual happiness, "Hey Joseph."

Joseph replies, happy to hear Kristen's voice, "Kristen, what a nice surprise."

Kristen speaks cheerfully, "I just had to call. I have good news."

Joseph replies, "What is it?"

Kristen tells him, "I got the accountant position at Teller and Associates. Isn't that great?"

Joseph smiles to himself, "That's wonderful. I knew you would get the job."

Kristen replies, still in a happy mood, "Looks like we both hit the work force since you got that position with Toys For Tots."

Joseph chuckles at Kristen's jubilance, "It looks like everything is working out."

Kristen jubilantly replies, "I know. Isn't it awesome."

The conversation continues for a few more minutes, then they both hang up. As Joseph returns to his cleaning, he can't believe how well everything is going. Then, out of the blue, a horrible image crosses his mind. He sees the headstone's of his biological parents and his sister, and next to them is another headstone with Kristen's name on it. The image stops him dead in his tracks and a visible look of sickness crosses his face. Joseph does his best to push the horrible images from his mind, but they still linger.

DATE - June 10th, 1997
San Francisco, CA

It is a hot summer night in the big city. In a dark, downtown alley with the crazy sounds of the city echoing in the distance, two of Papa Martoni's men flank a young man on his knees. The young man is dressed in slacks, shirt and tie and his hands are tied behind his back. Varges and Daniel walk up. They are both dressed in their usual suits and Varges has his shoulder length black hair pulled back in a ponytail.

The young man begs, "Please Mr. Martoni, don't kill me. I didn't know I was working in your area."

Varges shakes his head and puts on a pair of black gloves, "We run all of San Francisco. Everyone knows that. So you must have intruded on purpose."

The young man pleads, "It will never happen again."

Varges looks at Daniel, "He is right about that."

Daniel smiles at Varges as Varges pulls out his 9mm pistol.

The man begs one last time, "Please."

Varges replies by putting one bullet right between the young man's eyes.

Varges holsters his pistol, "Dump the body."

As the two men grab the body, Varges and Daniel turn and walk off.

DATE - July 2nd, 1997
San Francisco, CA

Kristen and Joseph are sitting at a desk in one of the city's numerous Hallmark Stores. Kristen, in some loose fitting shorts and t-shirt with the bear claw necklace hanging around her neck, is looking over some wedding invitations. Joseph, in jean shorts and t-shirt, stares at Kristen, still not able to completely shake the image of the headstone.

Kristen looks over at Joseph and can tell something is wrong by the look on his face, "Is everything okay? You've been distant all day."

Joseph does his best to give a reassuring smile, "Yea, I'm okay."

Joseph doesn't want Kristen to know about the images he saw in his head. He can tell by the look on Kristen's face that his answer wasn't too reassuring.

At that moment, the saleswoman walks up, "Can I help you with anything?"

Kristen returns her thoughts to the wedding and replies, "Yes. If we order the invitations today, how long will it take to get them?"

The saleswoman thinks for a second, "It takes about four weeks."

Kristen looks at Joseph, "That will give us plenty of time to mail them out and get the replies."

Joseph smiles at the saleswoman, "Thank you."

The saleswoman walks off.

Joseph doesn't want Kristen to think about what is going on with him so he picks up one of the invitations, "What do you think about this one? I think it would look really good with the colors we have chosen."

Kristen nods, "That's the one I've been leaning towards." She glances over the invitations on the desk again, "Yea, I think we should go with that one."

Joseph puts his arm around Kristen, "Alright, one thing down, a million more to go."

Kristen laughs at Joseph, "And next on the agenda is the cake and the possible locations."

The two of them go to find the saleswoman so they can put in their order for the invitations. Joseph lovingly watches as Kristen works out the order with the saleswoman. Joseph can't believe how in love with Kristen he is.

DATE - August 1st, 1997
San Francisco, CA

The only light in the studio apartment is the soft glow of candles on the new dinner table Joseph recently added to his apartment. Soft music plays in the background. Joseph and Kristen are enjoying their candlelight dinner. Kristen is wearing a nice v-neck top and tight fitting designer jeans with her hair pulled back into a ponytail. Joseph is wearing a designer shirt and designer jeans.

Joseph puts down his glass of tea, "Well, it's getting closer to the big day. November is not that far off."

Kristen smiles and decides to play with Joseph some, "Yep, you're not getting cold feet are you?"

Joseph playfully replies, "Well, you know, it is a big step and it is a major change in life. Plus, I'm kind of use to living alone."

Kristen gives him a you better not be serious look, "Oh really."

Joseph smiles at her response, "There is no way I would ever back out of marrying you."

Kristen gives him a loving smile. Once dinner is over they get up and slow dance to one of their favorite songs playing on the radio.

Joseph stares into Kristen's eyes, "You are so beautiful."

Kristen speaks softly, "Joseph." She gives him a sly smile, "Take me to bed or lose me forever."

Joseph lovingly stares at Kristen as he picks her up and carries her off. He puts her down next to the bed and they start kissing and exploring each other with their hands. Joseph removes Kristen's shirt and sees the bear claw hanging around her neck. Kristen smiles at him.

Joseph smiles back, "I love you."

Once again they share their love for each other and once it's over, they drift off to dream.

DATE - September 3rd, 1997
San Francisco, CA

Varges, wearing a muscle shirt and swim trunks, is sitting in a lounge chair on the back patio of the Martoni home. He is enjoying the wonderful day with a drink and some sun. Varges is talking on his cell phone.

Varges speaks into his cell phone, "The deal will go down at 9 pm on the 28th, the docks by Fisherman's Wharf, dock 12, pier 4."

A man's voice responds, "Are you sure the dock will be clear then?"

Varges smirks, "Don't worry. Everything will be fine."

The man replies, "I don't want any problems. An exchange of this size can give me a lot of time."

Varges reassures the man, "Hey, it's taken care of. There is nothing to worry about."

Each man hangs up. Daniel, wearing his swimming attire, walks over to Varges.

Varges smiles at Daniel, "Everything is set. Make sure the men know what to do."

Daniel nods, "I've already informed them. All we need to do now is wait for the day to get here."

Varges puts his sunglasses on, "Good."

Daniel walks off and Varges smiles to himself as he thinks about the upcoming exchange.

DATE - September 28th, 1997
San Francisco, CA

The ringing phone echoes through Joseph's apartment and after the fifth ring, Joseph's answering machine picks up, "Hello. This is Joseph Thompson, please leave a message."

Kristen's voice, "Hey Joseph, I guess you're working late. I'll be waiting for you at my parent's boat. I have some chores to do there. I love you. Bye."

Kristen, wearing tight fitting jeans, long sleeve t-shirt and as always, the bear claw necklace with her hair in a ponytail, hangs up and heads off for her parent's boat.

Joseph walks into his apartment. He puts his keys down on the counter next to the phone and he notices he has a message. He pushes the playback button. Joseph smiles at Kristen's voice. He looks at his watch and it shows 7:40 pm. He gets cleaned up, dressed in jeans and a long sleeve t-shirt and heads for his motorcycle.

Kristen has just finished cleaning up the living area of the boat when she hears some faint noise coming from the dock. She looks at her watch and it shows 8:45 pm. She smiles and figures it is Joseph having trouble with the gate or something. Kristen makes her way off the boat and walks down the pier towards the dock. She stops at the end of the pier when she sees ten men in nice suits standing around another man in a suit that is on his knees. She watches in horror as Varges shoots the man that was on his knees, but she doesn't hear the gunshot.

Kristen is terrified and she takes a couple of steps back. Suddenly, a big man in a nice suit that appears to be in his thirties, grabs her from behind. Kristen struggles, but the man is just too big and strong. The man carries Kristen in a bear hug over to the other men as Kristen continues to struggle.

The man puts Kristen down, but keeps her in a bear hug, "Varges, look what I found."

Varges looks over and sees the man holding Kristen, "Well, it looks like we have a problem."

At that time, they all hear a motorcycle in the distance. Kristen knows it has to be Joseph. She remembers some of the things Joseph has shown her and she slowly works her right hand down to her thigh near the man's private area.

The man speaks again, "What should we do with her?"

Varges replies coldly, "No witnesses."

Kristen's face gets a look of worry as she doesn't like the sound of that. Joseph parks his motorcycle and heads for the gate completely unaware of what is going on.

Varges looks at Kristen, "What's your name young lady? I always like to know who it is that I kill."

Kristen responds by hitting the man that is holding her in his private area. The man grunts, lets go of Kristen and doubles over. Kristen runs as fast as she can for the gate. It is only fifty yards away and she sees Joseph opening the gate. Joseph sees Kristen running at him and he can tell something is wrong, then he sees the other men on the dock.

Kristen screams, "Joseph!"

Varges takes aim at Kristen and pulls the trigger. The bullet hits Kristen in the lower back and exits her stomach. Joseph gets a look of disbelief as everything seems to be moving in slow motion to him. He looks at the man who just shot the woman he loves and he sees Varges Martoni's face clearly.

As Kristen falls, Joseph yells, "Kristen!"

Daniel, who is standing next to Varges, shoots at Joseph. Joseph falls, taking a flesh wound to the leg.

Then, Daniel hears sirens in the background, "Varges, it's the cops, we have to get out of here."

Varges puts his pistol away, "We have to make sure their dead."

Daniel puts his pistol away, "We don't have time. If we wait too much longer we won't be able to sneak pass the incoming police cars."

Varges looks towards Joseph and Kristen. He doesn't see any movement.

Varges nods, "Okay, lets get out of here."

The Martoni squad runs off away from where Joseph and Kristen are laying. As soon as the men disappear, Joseph crawls over to Kristen.

Joseph kneels next to Kristen, holding her head up with his right hand as he places his left hand on top of her hands that are on her stomach, "Oh God, Kristen."

Kristen speaks in a weak tone, "Joseph, I'm, I'm ..."

Kristen is unable to finish the sentence.

Tears come to Joseph's eyes as he speaks, "You're going to make it. Just hang on."

Kristen coughs a little blood, "I'm not sure."

Joseph shakes his head, not wanting to hear that, "Kristen, stay with me." He chokes back some tears, "You can't go, I need you."

Kristen reaches up with her left hand and weakly touches Joseph's cheek, smearing a little blood on him, "Promise me something."

Joseph nods trying to stay strong and not cry, "Anything my love."

Kristen speaks as her voice gets weaker, "If I don't make it, every year on my birthday, light a candle to remember me and my love for you." She lets out another cough, "My eternal love with an eternal flame."

Joseph chokes back more tears, "You're going to make it. Just hold on."

The sirens are getting closer, but Joseph is oblivious to his surroundings as his full focus is on Kristen.

Kristen's voice is even weaker, "Promise me."

Joseph closes his eyes as a couple of tears roll down his cheek. He knows he is about to lose Kristen.

Joseph opens his eyes and stares as lovingly as he can at Kristen, "I promise."

Kristen manages a slight smile, "I ..."

Before she can finish her words, the last breath leaves Kristen's body. The tears run freely down Joseph's face.

Joseph gently kisses her lips and looks up, "Why God, why?!"

Joseph closes his eyes and the only thing he can see is the face of the man who killed Kristen. All he can see is the face of Varges Martoni.

DATE - October 1st, 1997
San Francisco, CA

It is an overcast fall afternoon. The ground is still damp from the morning rain and the temperature has risen into the low seventies. Detective Jackson, along with three uniformed police officers, knocks on the front door of the Martoni home.

The man that was holding Kristen at the docks answers the door, "Can I help you?"

Detective Jackson holds up his badge, "I'm Detective Jackson with the San Francisco Police Department, we are here to speak with Varges Martoni."

The man waves them in, "Wait here in the foyer. I'll get him."

The officers and Detective Jackson walk into the foyer as the man goes to get Varges.

Detective Jackson speaks quietly to the officers, "Stay ready. Anything can happen when this goes down."

A couple of minutes later, Varges, dressed in his usual suit, and the man who answered the door walk up and Varges smiles, "Detective Jackson, how can I help you?"

Detective Jackson pulls out a piece of paper, "Varges Martoni, I have a warrant for your arrest. The charge is murder in the second degree. You are going to have to come with us."

Varges looks at the man next to him. Detective Jackson and the officers are prepared for trouble.

Varges speaks calmly to the man, "Tell my father what is going on." He looks at Detective Jackson, "Shall we."

Detective Jackson motions to one of the officers and the officer cuffs Varges. Detective Jackson and the officers walk out with Varges as the man goes to find Papa Martoni and tell him what has happened.

DATE - October 5th, 1997
San Francisco, CA

It is an overcast fall day at Parkview Cemetery. A light drizzle is in the air as Kristen's funeral service is just about over. The priest finishes his speech. William and Becky Shobe are joined by Mr. and Mrs. Lee and Joseph by Kristen's casket. The other family and friends watch as Joseph lays a single red rose on the casket. Once the service is over, the other guests give their condolences to William, Becky and Joseph.

Everyone starts to make their way to their cars, leaving William, Becky, Joseph, Mr. and Mrs. Lee by the gravesite.

Mr. Lee places his hand on Joseph's shoulder, "How are you doing my son?"

Joseph is unable to answer, but he slightly nods.

William looks at Joseph, "It's not your fault Joe. There is nothing you could have done."

This time Joseph manages a couple words, "I know."

William and Becky each hug Joseph and they walk off with Mr. and Mrs. Lee. Joseph just stares at the casket and tears come to his eyes. He closes his eyes and replays the night over in his mind. Each time he sees the images, his anger for Varges Martoni grows.

Joseph opens his eyes and looks at the casket as it lowers into the ground, "The man responsible will pay, and I'll never forget my promise."

Joseph stands there for a few more minutes and then turns to leave. He sees Detective Jackson get into his car and drive off.

Joseph looks back at the grave and places his right hand to his heart, "I'll miss you so much and I'll always love you."

As Joseph turns away from the grave, he drops his right hand from his heart and makes a motion like he tossed his heart towards the casket. Joseph takes a deep breath and finally walks off.

DATE - December 1st, 1997
San Francisco, CA

It is a cold day in the city. A female reporter about 5'4" tall and weighing about 125 pounds is standing in front of the courthouse. She is wearing a blue female suit, a winter cap covering her black hair and a winter coat.

The female reporter looks into her camera with her dark brown eyes, "Good Morning San Francisco. This is Eileen Morgan and I'm here at City Hall. In a few minutes the murder trial of Varges Martoni will begin."

She looks over and sees Joseph walking up the steps. Eileen and her camera man walk over to Joseph.

Eileen speaks to Joseph, "Mr. Thompson, could you tell us how you feel about Varges Martoni and this trial?"

Joseph speaks solemnly, "Varges Martoni will pay for his crime and I have confidence in the police and the DA that they will convict him. Now, please excuse me."

Eileen looks back at the camera, "This is Eileen Morgan for Channel 6 News. We will keep you up to date as new information emerges from the trial. Have a good morning San Francisco."

Joseph shakes his head as he enters the front door. He just wants justice to be done and to be left alone.

DATE - December 23rd, 1997
San Francisco, CA

The courtroom is packed full of law enforcement and citizens. This is the day everyone has been waiting on. It was a quick trial, which surprised everyone, and now they await the verdict. Joseph, wearing jeans and a long sleeve shirt, sits next to Detective Jackson, who is wearing his usual work suit, in the front row right behind the DA, an average sized African-American man in his mid-forties.

The courtroom gets quiet as the judge looks at the head juror, "Has the jury reached a verdict?"

The juror stands, "We have your honor."

The judge looks over at Varges, "The defense will stand."

Varges and his lawyer rise to their feet with a look of complete confidence.

The judge speaks, "Please read the verdict."

Everyone in the courtroom holds their breath in anticipation. Detective Jackson just knows that this verdict is going to be the first step in bringing down the Martoni house of cards.

The juror opens the paper in his hand and speaks, "We the jury find the defendant, Varges Martoni, on the count of murder in the second degree." A pause, "Not guilty."

Joseph's head drops. He can't believe what he just heard. He watched this man kill Kristen and now the man will go free. Joseph's anger starts to grow. Detective Jackson has a look of disbelief as he can't believe it has happened again.

The judge speaks, "Let the record show, not guilty. Mr. Martoni, you are free to go." He bangs his gavel, "This court is adjourned."

Varges, Papa Martoni, Daniel and the lawyer start to celebrate. The DA walks out stunned.

Joseph looks at Detective Jackson, "You call this justice?!"

Detective Jackson sighs, "The system doesn't always work, believe me, but it's the only system we have."

Joseph stands, "To hell with the system!"

Joseph walks towards Varges. Detective Jackson moves quickly and restrains Joseph a couple of feet from Varges.

Varges smiles at Joseph, "Sorry friend. You win some and you lose some. I guess you should learn how to better choose your fights."

Joseph shakes his head and replies with anger, "You might win for now, but this fight isn't over." He pauses as he remembers the words of his biological father, "You should never stop fighting until the fight is done."

Detective Jackson finally pulls Joseph out of the courtroom. Varges smiles and thinks nothing of Joseph's words. However, Papa Martoni has a look of concern on his face over what Joseph said.

Detective Jackson lets go of Joseph in the hallway, "Look, it's not over. We will go back to the case files and see what other leads we have. I'm not giving up on this."

Joseph mumbles under his breath as he turns and walks off, "Like the police or anyone else is going to do anything."

Joseph walks off. He can't believe how something like this can happen and how it needs to be made right.

Chapter 8

DATE - December 24th, 1997
San Francisco, CA

It is a cold winter day in the city. A layer of snow and ice covers the ground and a light snowfall is in the afternoon air. The temperature has dropped to the upper twenties.

Ever since the verdict, Joseph has walked the streets. He has no destination in mind and doesn't care where his feet take him. He replays the good old days with Kristen in his mind. No matter how many times he goes over it, the outcome is still the same. Kristen is gone and all that's left is Varges Martoni's face. With each replay, his anger burns him up inside. All Joseph can think about is how to make things right.

Joseph passes other couples on the street. The other couples seem so happy. Seeing others in love makes the pain in his heart unbearable, but no more tears run. All that seems to run through his mind is revenge. He knows that he must make things right, there is no other way. His mind, heart and soul won't rest until it is right again.

Jody Slyman

DATE - December 25th, 1997
San Francisco, CA

The snow has stopped, but it is a white Christmas in the city. The evening temperature has dropped into the low twenties. Joseph has not been home in two days, nor has he seen or spoken to anyone. One thing he has noticed while walking the streets is that there has been fewer people out than he would have figured for this time of the year. It is Christmas time, but it seems like nobody feels safe going outside.

Joseph can understand why people would feel that way, how could they feel safe when the city watches the system that is meant to protect them fail, when someone can commit murder and not be punished. Joseph's wandering feet carries him into the park and he hears Christmas carols being sang in the distance.

Joseph walks up to a small group of people watching a young choir as they finish Frosty the Snowman. The next song the choir starts to sing is Silent Night.

Halfway through the song, Joseph hears Kristen's voice, "It's time Joseph. Time to make things right."

Suddenly, an idea pops into Joseph's mind. An idea on how to make things right, on how he can get to Varges Martoni. He knows that once Varges is dead, everything will be right again.

Joseph nods slightly and speaks quietly to himself, not sure of why he is thinking the words in his mind, "Silent Night."

Joseph heads for his apartment, thinking about his plan the entire way.

DATE - January 2nd, 1998
San Francisco, CA

It is a freezing cold winter day. The snow continues to fall and the frigid air continues to blow across the bay. Joseph, bundled up from the cold, is standing in a grove of trees near the bank of the bay. He watches on as law enforcement works on pulling his GTO out of the bay. Joseph knows that during this time of the year, they will have trouble finding a body in the bay.

Joseph smiles to himself, "Part one of the plan is in place."

Joseph turns around and walks over to his motorcycle. He has removed his plates and registration sticker from his bike and painted the bike all black. Joseph knows that if he stays to the side streets and alleys, he should be able to avoid the police. He gets on his bike and makes his way back to his apartment. Joseph sneaks into his apartment so no one would see him. He grabs his backpack full of clothes and disappears.

While Joseph disappears into the night, Mr. and Mrs. Lee turn on the news and so does William and Becky Shobe. They see Eileen Morgan standing near the bay with a bunch of police cars behind her.

Eileen Morgan reports, "Just about thirty minutes ago, law enforcement was able to pull a car that crashed into the bay out of the water. The police are not releasing the name of the owner at this time until they have informed the family. Now, we have been told that the police have not found a body at this time, but the search continues. We will report more on this breaking story as we receive the information."

The camera pans over and Mr. and Mrs. Lee and William and Becky see the GTO in the background. They know right away it is Joseph's car.

Mrs. Lee gasps, "Oh dear God."

At that moment, the doorbell rings. Mr. Lee gets up and answers the door. All their questions are answered when Mr. Lee sees two police officers standing there.

DATE - January 10th, 1998
San Francisco, CA

In the darkness of the cold winter night. Joseph returns to the old, abandoned downtown church after collecting the last of his food and water supplies. He walks into the room that was at one time where the priest would have slept. Joseph looks at the various gear he has laying on the old, rundown desk. He has one GLOC 36 pistol with three loaded magazines and five hundred extra rounds. He has one SOG combat knife and two throwing knives, one for each boot.

Joseph looks at the black, nylon holster and double magazine holder that he plans on wearing on his right hip. He looks at the knife sheath he modified so he can carry the combat knife horizontally on his left hip. Last, he looks over the two throwing knife sheathes that he can lace into his boots.

Joseph looks over the outfit he has come up with. He has all black infantry combat boots. He has black SWAT trousers, that he will blouse just above his boots and black boot socks. He has a black, skin tight, long sleeve shirt, gray nomex pilot gloves and a black mask that only has an opening across his eyes. He has a charcoal gray trench coat and fedora hat.

Joseph nods his approval and walks back out into the main room of the abandoned church and looks around. He knows it will be a good base of operations.

Joseph speaks to himself, "Now all that is left is to gather information on the Martoni family."

DATE - February 1st, 1998
San Francisco, CA

Varges Martoni is standing next to his car outside the Martoni home in the cold and overcast early morning.

Papa Martoni walks up, "It has to be this way Varges. Just lay low until the heat from the trial goes away."

Varges replies, "I understand father. Keep me up on how things are going. When you think the time is right for me to return, just say the word."

Papa Martoni smiles, "I will. Just watch your back in Chicago. We have enemies there."

Varges nods, "I will father."

Varges hugs his father and gets into the car. Papa Martoni watches the car drive off with his son. A few hours later, Varges' flight lands safely in Chicago.

As the sun starts to set, Joseph gets dressed in his vigilante outfit. He has a focused look in his eyes, a look of revenge. Joseph walks to the back door of the church that leads to the alley. He uncovers his bike that he has sitting near the back door and pushes it out into the alley. Joseph gets on his bike and starts it up. He takes off down the alley. On his way to the better part of San Francisco, where the Martoni's live, he passes numerous gangs, drug dealers, drug houses and hookers. He can only think about how much things need to change.

Papa Martoni is sitting on the back patio of his home talking with Daniel and getting some fresh air. Joseph rides up towards the back of the Martoni home. He stops about a quarter mile from the back wall and hides his bike in some bushes. Joseph quietly works his way up to the back wall that blocks the rest of the world from the Martoni home. Joseph quickly scales the ten foot concrete wall and lands without a sound on the opposite side. Joseph manages to sneak all the way up to the bushes just 25 feet to the right of Papa Martoni and Daniel.

Papa Martoni speaks to Daniel unaware anyone is watching or listening, "Varges made it safely to Vito's home. Keep him in the loop while he is laying low."

Daniel nods, "I will Papa."

Papa Martoni and Daniel walk back into the house. Joseph can't believe what he just heard. He doesn't want to believe that Varges is gone. Joseph quietly works his way back to the back wall. He scales the wall and makes his way back to his motorcycle.

As Joseph starts his motorcycle, he whispers to himself, "I don't believe it. How can I make things right now?" He pauses, "With Varges gone, maybe I should end this vigilante idea before something bad happens."

He turns his bike around and starts back towards the church.

DATE - February 2nd, 1998
San Francisco, CA

Joseph rides through the cold 2 am city streets and alleys. When he gets about six blocks from the church, he sees a young, white teenage girl run into an alley ahead of him being chased by three teenage, white boys. Joseph slowly rides up and turns into the alley. He parks his motorcycle just inside the alley. He gets off his bike and he can hear muffled screams coming from further down the alley. Joseph quietly makes his way towards the noises.

Joseph stops in the shadows about twenty feet from the three boys and the girl. The girl is laying on her back off to the left side of the alley. One boy is holding her right arm down and another is holding her left arm down. The third boy is laying on top of her, his right hand is trying to take her pants off and his left hand covers her mouth. The girl's jacket is open and her blouse is ripped open and she is struggling to keep the boy on top of her from being able to get her pants off of her. Joseph has seen enough.

The boy on top of the girl speaks, "One of you cover her mouth so I can get her pants off."

Neither of the other two boys move. The kid looks up at his friends and he notices that they are staring at something behind him. The kid turns his head to see what it is. He sees the masked person standing five feet behind him.

The kid laying on top of the girl speaks, "Just who do you think you are?"

Joseph replies in monotone, "Rape is wrong. It is a crime."

The kid replies, trying to act tough, "Beat it freak before something happens to you."

Joseph replies again in monotone, "What you three are doing is unacceptable and you should be punished." Joseph pulls out his pistol with his right hand, "And the only acceptable punishment is death."

The three kids scramble to their feet with extreme fear in their faces. Joseph can see the girl clearly now and she can't be any older than fifteen. He stares at the three young men in disgust.

The leader holds up his hands as he shakes with fear, "Take it easy man. We were just trying to scare her, we weren't going to do anything."

Joseph points the GLOC at the leader, "Too late young man."

Two rounds ring out and the young man falls in a pool of blood. The other two boys watch in horror as their friend falls. Then, four more shots and the other two boys join their friend. Joseph reloads his pistol, then holsters it.

Joseph walks over and helps the shocked girl to her feet, "Are you okay?"

The girl is shaking and staring at nothing, "I think so."

Joseph walks the dazed girl back to his motorcycle.

Joseph pulls out a bottle of water from the compartment under his seat, "Here, drink some of this."

The young girl takes the bottle of water, "Thanks."

After she drinks some of the water, Joseph speaks, "I can take you to the police. They can help you more than I can."

The young girl nods, still a little shocked, "Okay." She climbs on with Joseph and they head off down the alley, passing the three bodies. Joseph stops about a block away from a police station. The girl climbs off.

She looks at Joseph, "Thanks for helping me." She finally has to ask, "Who are you?"

Joseph lets out a pleased sigh, "Silent Knight."

Joseph turns his motorcycle around and rides off into the darkness of the early morning. The girl walks into the police station.

The police officer at the reception desk looks up at the young girl, "Can I help you miss?"

The young girl explains everything that happened with the boys and the masked vigilante.

When she is finished, the officer sits back, "You expect me to believe that?"

The girl raises her voice, obviously upset, "I'm telling you the truth!"

The outburst catches the attention of Detective Jackson who just walked in for an early start on the day. Detective Jackson would normally let the officer handle something like this, but something tells him to stop.

Detective Jackson walks over to the young girl, "Is there something wrong young lady?"

The young girl tells her story to Detective Jackson. Detective Jackson listens intently, but he is having a hard time believing it.

The girl can tell that Detective Jackson doesn't believe her, "I can show you where the bodies are at."

Detective Jackson nods, "Okay, lets go."

The young girl follows Detective Jackson to his car and they get in. She explains the way as Detective Jackson drives. They finally reach the alley. Detective Jackson drives down the alley. He stops the car as soon as his headlights reveal the three dead bodies.

The girl smiles, "I told you so."

Detective Jackson radios in the location. The two of them get out of the car and walk a little closer to the bodies.

Detective Jackson shakes his head, "I'm sorry I didn't believe you." He looks at the girl, "Who did you say did this?"

The girl answers, "He called himself Silent Knight."

Detective Jackson looks back at the bodies, "What is going on?"

As Detective Jackson starts working the crime scene, Joseph walks into the main room of the abandoned church and removes his fedora and mask. He looks up at the cross and replays what happened in his mind.

He speaks out loud to himself, "It has gone too far. I have to stop it now before it is too late."

Joseph hears Kristen's voice, "You did the right thing Joseph. You saved that girl."

Joseph looks left and sees Kristen standing there, not ten feet away, "But I killed those boys."

Kristen smiles, "They were rapists and they deserved it. All criminals deserve to die. If you don't do it, then who will?"

Joseph gets a faraway look in his eyes as he remembers the verdict from the trial, "You're right."

Kristen replies, "Make them pay Joseph, make them all pay."

Kristen's image fades away and all that is left is the image of two crossed, silver swords on a black background. A couple seconds later, that image vanishes and Joseph is alone.

Joseph looks back at the cross, "Okay then, it's time for all the criminals to pay."

DATE - February 4th, 1998

San Francisco, CA

In the early morning hours of the new day, Detective Jackson is sitting at his desk looking over the file on the three dead rapists.

Detective Jackson speaks to himself, "Silent Knight. Are you real, and if so, who are you?"

Detective Jackson continues to flip through the crime scene photos. He wonders how good the description of the Silent Knight is that the girl gave them. He knows that the girl was in shock and it could have caused her to fantasize some of what happened. However, he knows that he has to go with what the young girl has given him because she is the only eye witness.

Detective Jackson sighs and poses a question to himself, "Why would he brutally gun down three boys, then give the girl a ride to the police station? It just doesn't make sense."

Detective Jackson continues through the file. He sighs at the lack of evidence.

Detective Jackson puts the file down and rubs his eyes, "There is even less here than a Martoni crime scene."

Detective Jackson stretches his arms and prepares himself for a long day.

Detective Jackson sighs, "This one is going to be tough, but something tells me, I'll get another scene to look at soon." He looks back at the pictures on his desk, "Silent Knight, who are you?"

DATE - February 14th, 1998
San Francisco, CA

It's a cold morning as patches of snow covers the ground. The morning temperature has risen into the low thirties. Joseph is standing in the Parkview Cemetery, by a large tree near Kristen's grave. Joseph watches as an early mourner leaves the cemetery. He is wearing his Silent Knight outfit except for his mask and gloves. He has added one thing to his outfit. On the left breast of his trench coat, he has a patch of two crossed, silver swords on a black background. He got five hundred of them and it wasn't easy to get them without being seen. He plans on leaving one at every crime scene so they will know that the Silent Knight is responsible.

Seeing that the cemetery is empty now, Joseph walks over to Kristen's grave. He pulls a candle and matches out of his jacket pocket. He places the candle on Kristen's headstone and lights it.

Joseph speaks to the headstone, "I promised, and here I am my love. I miss you so much, but I know you can see me and hear me. We will be together again one day."

As Joseph turns to leave, he hears Kristen's voice, "I love you Joseph."

As Joseph walks off, he smiles to himself and thinks, it is time to make a stand, to fight for what is right.

Chapter 9

DATE - February 21st, 1998
San Francisco, CA

Joseph slowly rides through the alleys and side streets in the middle of the cold, dark night. The hustle and bustle of the big city is mainly that of the street people and gangs at this time of night, but a few other citizens have wandered out into the dangerous environment. Joseph is looking for anything to get involved with and after another hour he sees what he has been looking for.

Joseph watches as a car with three young men, obviously gang members by the way they are dressed, slowly drives by a local liquor store. Joseph sees two other young men standing outside the front of the liquor store and they too appear to be wearing gang colors, but Joseph also can see a young couple just start to walk out of the liquor store. A young couple that is about to be in the wrong place at the wrong time.

The two young men standing in front of the liquor store sees the car, but it is too late. The two young men reach under their jackets as two automatic weapons appear out the window of the slow moving car. Suddenly, the two

123

automatic weapons reign bullets at the people standing around the front of the store. The two young rival gang members fall in the hail of gunfire, but so does the innocent couple out getting a bottle of wine for their anniversary. The car speeds away and Joseph follows the fast moving car for about a mile.

Joseph watches from a half block away as the car pulls into a poorly lit, empty parking lot. Joseph pulls into a nearby alley and parks his motorcycle. He uses the shadows and noises of the city night to cover his movement as he makes his way towards the car on foot.

The driver, a young African-American in his late teens, puts the car in park, "I got to piss, hang on."

The driver gets out and walks pass the back of the car to the other side of the vacant parking lot.

A couple minutes pass and the guy in the passenger seat, a white teenage boy, yells out the window, "Hurry up man, we don't have all night."

The guy in the back seat, another young white teen, looks out the back window. He sees the driver laying on the ground facing away from them.

The guy in the back seat chuckles, "I think he got too juiced and passed out. Lets go get him."

The two teens get out of the car and walk towards the driver.

The kid from the backseat yells, "Hey man, get up!"

Despite the yelling, the driver doesn't respond. The driver is laying on his side facing away from them as the two young men walk up. The young man from the passenger seat squats next to the driver while the other kid stands just to the left of his friend.

The kid rolls the driver to his back, "Hey man, get up."

The two young men freeze in fear when they see the pool of blood on the pavement and they see the driver's throat has been cut. Suddenly, the young man squatting is kicked to the ground and the other young man feels the cold steel blade of a knife driven into the right side of his neck. As Joseph removes the knife from the young man's neck, the kid falls and he is dead before he hits the ground. The last gang member looks up and sees the Silent Knight standing over him. In a panic, the gang member reaches under his coat looking for a gun, but pulls a knife instead. Joseph quickly brings his right leg around and kicks the knife out of the young man's hand.

Joseph stares at the young man, slowly putting his knife away and pulling out his pistol, "What you three did was cold blooded murder and now you must die."

The gang member holds up his hands, unable to move any other part of his body due to sheer terror. Two shots ring out in the night and the last gang member is dead. Joseph puts his pistol away and pulls a patch out of his jacket pocket. He drops the patch next to the bodies and disappears into the darkness of the night.

DATE - March 14th, 1998
San Francisco, CA

The sun has set and the night has come to life in the downtown area of the city. Chad McKeenan, a stout young man of 6' tall and 200 pounds with short blond hair and blue eyes, walks out of the movies with his girlfriend, Rena, a beautiful young 5'6" 130 pound redhead with green eyes.

Chad looks around, "I didn't think the movie was that long. Stay close to me Rena." He glances around again, "I hate being out in this part of town at this time of night."

Rena hugs his arm as they start off for their car which is parked two blocks away from the movie theatre. As they pass the first alley, four young Hispanic men step out, each one wearing a different color of bandana. The four young men are members of one of the more prominent gangs in the city.

The kid wearing a red bandana pulls out a .38 caliber revolver, "Don't make a noise and get in the alley."

The four young men are smiling, knowing that they have pulled this off numerous times before, but what they didn't know is that this time was going to be different. Joseph watches the four gang members from the nearby shadows. He started following the four men an hour ago. He had a hunch they would cause trouble.

Chad and Rena do as they are told, not wanting to upset the four young men in any way. They stop about halfway down the alley next to a group of dumpsters. A young man with a green bandana takes Chad's wallet and Rena's purse.

Chad speaks shakily, "Take the money. We won't say anything, just don't hurt us."

A teenage kid with a black bandana punches Chad in the gut and Chad drops to his knees.

Rena moves her attention to her boyfriend with a look of concern, "Chad."

The four gang members turn their attention to Rena. It becomes obvious to anyone that is watching that this is going to be more than a simple robbery.

Out of nowhere, the kid with the red bandana feels someone grab his hand holding the pistol. The kid feels a quick jerk and twist and his wrist snaps. The pistol falls to the ground, and the kid quickly follows. The kid wearing a white bandana looks over in time to feel the hardened steel of a throwing knife hit him in the chest, just above his sternum and he falls to the pavement as the life runs out of his body. The kid with the green bandana turns and takes a quick swing at the stranger that just appeared amongst them. The kid feels a hand grab his arm and spin him around. The young man's head slams into one of the dumpsters sending him to the pavement. Before the kid with the black bandana can figure out what is going on, his feet are kicked out from under him and he lands hard on the pavement.

The kid with the red bandana reaches for his pistol, but Joseph kicks it away. Joseph quickly draws his combat knife and in one quick, deadly motion, he slices the kid with the red bandana's throat. The young man wearing the black bandana gets up and steps over by the masked vigilante. He throws a left hook at Joseph's head. Joseph ducks under the punch and drives his knife into the kid's chest just below the armpit, puncturing the kid's lung. As Joseph removes the knife, the kid drops. Joseph puts his knife away and pulls out his pistol. He turns back to the kid with the green bandana who is still shaking his head trying to get his wits back about him. Joseph aims at the last gang member.

The kid wearing the green bandana holds up his hands, and now on the receiving end of the violence, pleads and begs for his life, "Please don't kill me, please."

As Joseph pulls the trigger, he coldly says only one thing, "Kristen."

The deadly shot sends the last gang member to the pavement in a pool of blood. Joseph holsters his pistol and drops a patch by the body of the kid wearing the red bandana. Joseph retrieves his throwing knife and puts it back in his boot. Joseph looks over at Chad and Rena.

Chad manages to speak with a shaky voice, "Please man, don't hurt us."

Joseph just smiles to himself under his mask, turns and runs off into the night. Chad and Rena look at each other.

They both have a look on their faces of disbelief about what they just experienced.

DATE - March 18th, 1998

San Francisco, CA

In the morning hours of the new workday. Eileen Morgan is sitting in her car on the police parking lot. She is waiting for Detective Jackson to show up to work. After sitting there for a short time, she sees Detective Jackson pull onto the parking lot. Eileen gets out of her car as Detective Jackson parks his car. Detective Jackson gets out of his car and smiles as he sees Eileen Morgan walking towards him.

Eileen walks up to him, "Good morning detective."

Detective Jackson replies jokingly, "It was."

Eileen smiles, "Is that any way to speak to your favorite reporter?"

Detective Jackson sighs, "So, what can I do for you Miss Morgan?"

Eileen smiles, "I'm interested in the four bodies found the other night. I hear another patch was found."

Detective Jackson starts to walk off, "We're still investigating it. I have no comment."

Eileen hits him with the big question, "What about the Silent Knight?"

Detective Jackson walks back over to her, "I'll catch whoever it is leaving these patches, you can count on it."

Eileen replies, "Why are you the only one who seems to think the Silent Knight is real?"

Detective Jackson walks off, "Gut feeling Miss Morgan."

Silent Knight

In the darkness of the spring night in the city, Joseph has been following a car full of three of Papa Martoni's men for about thirty minutes now. Joseph knows that given the area of the city they are in, they have to be up to something. Joseph stays a block away from the car as it pulls into a huge parking lot with only one other car. Joseph gets off his bike and quietly makes his way towards the parking lot.

The three Martoni men get out of their car as a young oriental man gets out of the other car. The young oriental man has a briefcase in one hand and one of the Martoni men is also carrying a briefcase. Joseph watches from the shadows only twenty yards away as the young oriental man approaches the Martoni men. Joseph sees the oriental man exchange suitcases with the Martoni man.

The oriental man speaks to the Martoni men, "A pleasure to do business with you."

Joseph has seen all he can stand. Suddenly, three shots ring out and the oriental man's chest explodes. The Martoni men pull out their 9mm pistols as the oriental man hits the pavement. The three Martoni men look around, but the dark has impaired their vision. Three more shots ring out in the city night and one of the Martoni men falls in a pool of blood. As Joseph reloads his pistol, the last two Martoni men jump in their car and start it up. The driver puts the pedal on the floor and the car takes off. Two more shots come through the windshield and the driver slumps over. The car swerves and hits one of the light poles on the parking lot. The passenger steps out of the car obviously dazed as he sways back and forth and shakes his head. The man drops his pistol, then he feels a strong hand grab his shoulder and force him to his knees. Joseph steps around in front of the man.

The man blinks a few times when he sees the masked vigilante, "It's you, you're real."

Joseph aims his pistol at the man's head and speaks coldly, "Isn't this how it's done?"

The man replies with confidence, "Pull that trigger and you're a dead man. I ..."

Joseph interrupts with an uncaring tone, "I know you work for Papa Martoni and it really doesn't matter."

The man's face changes from confidence to fear as he realizes that this vigilante doesn't seem to fear the name of Papa Martoni. Joseph smiles beneath his mask as he pulls the trigger and watches the man's head explode. Joseph holsters his pistol, drops his patch and disappears into the streets.

DATE - May 22nd, 1998
San Francisco, CA

Joseph is sitting on the second story of a fire escape for an abandoned building. Joseph is enjoying the warmth of the city night. He continues to watch the alley that the fire escape drops into because he knows the alley is a place that numerous drug deals go down in. Joseph stands up in the shadows on the landing when he sees a woman, probably in her thirties and dressed in provocative clothing, leads two men, who look to be in their forties and dressed in nice business suits, into the alley. The lady and two men stop just under where Joseph is standing.

The lady pulls a small bag of white substance from the beltline of her skirt, "You got the money?"

The man standing to the lady's right reaches into his pants pocket, "Don't worry." He pulls out a small roll of money, "This should cover it."

The other man speaks up, "You know, if you want a little extra, we could have some fun right here."

The lady takes the money, "You're not really my type. I'm not into married men."

The man on the right speaks again, "I bet for the right amount of money, any man can be your type."

Joseph has seen and heard enough. Joseph hops over the railing and drops from the fire escape. He lands on the two men, knocking them to the ground as the lady takes a few steps back. As Joseph gets to his feet, the woman pulls a knife from her high heeled boot and swings it at Joseph. Joseph catches her arm, ducks underneath, twists the arm around and rams the knife into her chest. As she falls, Joseph turns to the two men.

The two men get to their knees and start pleading, "Please don't kill us."

Joseph shakes his head as he pulls out his pistol, "Two married men buying drugs and trying to have sex with a street woman in a dirty alley, please, at least try to die with a little dignity, since you're obviously not living with any."

The two men close their eyes. Six shots ring out, becoming another noise in the city night and both men lay dead. Joseph reloads his pistol, puts it away and drops a patch. He smiles under his mask, knowing Kristen would be proud of him.

DATE - June 28th, 1998
San Francisco, CA

In a dark and poorly lit residential area, Joseph is riding his motorcycle. He hears some distant screaming and yelling so he stops his motorcycle in some shadows near a group of bushes. His eyes catch some movement in front of a house just two houses up the street from where he is at. He sees a man standing on the bottom step of the porch yelling at a young woman holding a small child.

The young woman turns and walks away from the man. She is walking directly at Joseph. Joseph ducks deeper into the shadows as the woman approaches. As she gets near Joseph, the light from the nearby street pole lights up the woman's face. When the woman walks by, Joseph sees something that upsets him greatly. The woman's left eye is bruised and she has a bloody nose. Joseph looks back down the street and watches the man walk back into the house. His anger rises and Joseph knows that this must be dealt with.

As the man makes his drunken way into the kitchen to get another beer, Joseph quietly makes his way around to the back of the house. Joseph walks up on the back porch when he hears the man walking towards the back door. Joseph moves over into the shadows on the porch as the man opens the back door. The man walks out on the back porch completely unaware of the masked figure not more than ten feet away.

Joseph can see the bottle of beer in the man's right hand and he can smell the beer on the man's body. As the man raises the bottle up and tips his head back to take a drink, Joseph grabs the man's right wrist, twists it around and throws the man down on the porch.

Joseph speaks, "What you did is unforgivable."

The man speaks in a drunken voice, "Whoever you are, you're dead."

Joseph smiles, "Lets see what you got tough guy."

So drunk and not even realizing who he is facing, the man stands up and swings the beer bottle at Joseph. Joseph catches the man's arm and twists it. Joseph takes the bottle from the man and smashes it into the man's head. The bottle explodes and the man drops to his knees.

Joseph shakes his head, "Is that all you got?" He kicks the man in the back, sending the man to the porch again, "It's a lot different fighting someone who can fight back."

The man manages to get to his feet again and swings at Joseph. Joseph catches the arm again, turns and throws the man head first into a window. The window shatters with blood dripping everywhere. Joseph pulls the man out of the window and forces him to his knees.

Joseph pulls out his knife, "You're nothing but a pathetic drunk and a man who likes to beat on women."

At that moment, Joseph hears Kristen's voice, "Make him pay Joseph, make him pay."

Joseph smiles beneath his mask as he slowly cuts the man's throat. The man slumps over to the porch and blood runs out of his body. Joseph puts his knife away and drops his patch.

The next day Joseph reads an article in the paper and the article reports that the man had abused his girlfriend many times and that night he also raped her and hit the three year old child. The article also reports that the woman admitted that she returned the following morning with a gun, intending to kill the abusive man.

DATE - July 17th, 1998
San Francisco, CA

On a warm summer evening in the upper class part of town, two of Papa Martoni's men walk out of a nice Italian restaurant after having a good dinner. Both of the men were present at the docks the night Kristen was killed and both are unaware of the person that has been watching them all evening. They walk about half a block to a parking lot which has numerous cars, but no other people are present. They start walking towards a car on the right hand side of the parking lot and almost all the way to the back, near the alley.

The driver looks at the driver's side rear tire as they walk up, "Hey Tony, look at this."

Tony walks around the car, over to where the other man is at, "What is it Jimmy?"

The two men look down at the driver's side rear tire. The tire is flat and it looks like it has been slashed with a knife. As Tony prepares to say something, the two men hear the chambering of a round in a pistol behind them.

Joseph speaks, "Turn around, slowly."

The two men, unsure if they are the target of a hit or a random act of violence, do as they are told and they are now face to face with the Silent Knight.

Tony speaks with a little confidence, "Who the hell are you?"

Joseph smiles beneath his mask when he sees the men's faces, "I thought I recognized the two of you. Drop the hardware, slowly."

The two men know exactly what this masked man is talking about and they ever so slowly, remove their pistols and drop them on the pavement.

Joseph motions to the nearby alley with his pistol, "Lets go."

Tony and Jimmy glance at each other, both wondering what this vigilante has in mind.

As the three men walk into the alley, Joseph holsters his pistol, "I'm going to give the two of you more of a chance than you gave Kristen."

Tony and Jimmy look at each other as if to say, what is this man talking about?

When the three of them get halfway down the alley, Joseph stops, "This is far enough."

Tony and Jimmy stop. They turn to face the masked vigilante and notice that Joseph has put his pistol away.

Joseph raises his hands up to his waist, "Are you ready?"

Not sure exactly what is happening, but knowing they must do something or possibly die, the two men charge the Silent Knight. Joseph steps to his right and shoves Tony into Jimmy. Jimmy stumbles and falls to the pavement, but Tony keeps his balance. Tony turns and throws a left hook at Joseph. Joseph ducks under the punch and smashes Tony's left knee with his right foot. Tony screams in pain and as Tony drops to the pavement, Jimmy gets to his feet and charges at Joseph. Joseph turns his attention to Jimmy and realizes that Jimmy is nearly on top of him. Jimmy tackles Joseph to his back. Joseph quickly wraps his legs around Jimmy's body.

Jimmy, unskilled in martial arts and ground fighting, tries to raise his upper body away from Joseph. Joseph grabs Jimmy's left wrist and kicks his left leg up around Jimmy's neck. Before Jimmy can react, Joseph shifts all of his weight and straightens Jimmy's left arm until his left shoulder dislocates and his left elbow snaps. Joseph lets go as Jimmy screams in obvious pain.

Joseph stands up slowly as the two men lay on the ground, each holding their wounded limb. Joseph knows the fight is over so he pulls out his pistol. He turns to Tony and kills him with three shots to the chest. Joseph turns his attention to Jimmy.

Jimmy manages to speak through the pain, "Go ahead and kill me, but I have to know, who is Kristen?"

Joseph slowly aims in as pictures of Kristen's smiling face flash through his mind, "She was the most loving and wonderful woman in the world and you helped kill her."

Joseph puts two bullets into Jimmy's head, killing him. Joseph puts the GLOC away and drops his patch.

DATE - July 19th, 1998
San Francisco, CA

In the mid-afternoon hours of the incredibly hot summer day, Papa Martoni sits in his air conditioned den with Daniel and five other top men from his organization.

One middle aged man speaks, "This Silent Knight took out Tony and Jimmy. We have to do something."

Daniel shakes his head, "It is unfortunate, but there really isn't anything we can do. This Silent Knight is a ghost."

A different man, an older man, speaks, "That doesn't matter. We do it like in the old days. We put the word out on the streets and hunt him down."

Daniel chuckles at the older man's inability to let go of the ways of the past, "That will get us nowhere."

A third man, the youngest of the five, speaks up, "If we don't do something, everyone will think it is okay to take a shot at us. I think ..."

Papa Martoni who has been listening quietly, finally speaks up, "Dan is right. We can't rush into this. You men go and tell the others to be extra careful and to not go out in groups smaller than three men until I can come up with something." He looks over at Daniel, "Dan, you stay."

The five men walk out and Daniel questions, expecting Papa Martoni to have some sort of plan, "What do you want me to do?"

Papa Martoni sighs, "We stay away from this Silent Knight."

Daniel is taken completely off guard and gets a puzzled look on his face, "Mr. Martoni, are you sure?"

Papa Martoni nods and gives Daniel a most serious look, "This Silent Knight is real, and really good. If we go to war with him, we will lose much more than we can possibly gain. This is the first time I've ever felt this way Dan." He pauses as he nervously rubs his hands together, "I've never been scared before, but this Silent Knight scares me because I have no idea what he is after. We must avoid this man. Also, call Varges and let him know about Tony and Jimmy. Make sure he understands, he is not to return."

Daniel nods at Papa Martoni's wishes and leaves the room, not really believing what he just heard.

Chapter 10

DATE - August 4th, 1998
San Francisco, CA

As the clock creeps closer and closer to the noon hour, Detective Jackson sits at his desk going over all the case files on the Silent Knight, and he notices that there are quite a few of them. His captain has come down hard on him for not getting any closer to solving the case. His captain has even stuck him with a partner. His partner, Detective Daniels, is a new detective at that.

About that time, an attractive woman in her late twenties sits down at Detective Jackson's desk. She has short red hair, green eyes and holds a firm build of about 5'4" tall and 120 pounds. She is dressed in a gray female suit.

Detective Jackson looks at the woman, "Can I help you Miss?"

She smiles at him, "I'm your new partner, Detective Pamela Daniels."

Detective Jackson nods as if to say, I wasn't expecting a young, female partner.

Detective Daniels can tell that Detective Jackson is apprehensive, "I know. I'm young, female and not very experienced, but you know something, I am capable of the job. You see, these are the new days and we females actually have to meet the standards now."

Detective Jackson smiles. He can tell that he is going to like her, and her attitude.

Detective Jackson extends his right hand, "Sorry, I guess I forgot for a moment what it was like when I came up."

As they shake hands, Detective Jackson looks around and notices everyone is watching them.

Detective Jackson looks at his new partner, "Are you hungry?"

Detective Daniels nods, "A little."

Detective Jackson smiles, "Good, lets get out of here."

Detective Jackson takes her to a little out of the way diner.

As they walk into the diner, the owner, an older African-American man, greets his friend, "Darius, what you been up to?"

The two men shake hands and Detective Jackson replies, "I would like you to meet my new partner, Detective Pamela Daniels."

The owner shakes Detective Daniels' hand, "Well, aren't you just the prettiest thing these old eyes have seen."

Detective Daniels smiles, a little embarrassed, "Thank you. It's nice to meet you."

The owner looks back to Detective Jackson, "What can I get you my old friend?"

Detective Jackson smiles, "We will have two of the lunch specials and some coffee."

The owner nods, "Coming right up."

The owner walks off and the two detectives sit down in one of the open booths at the back of the diner.

Detective Jackson speaks, "So, have you had a chance to look at the case files?"

Detective Daniels nods, "Yes, I read over them a few days ago."

Detective Jackson leans forward, "What's your view of the case?"

Detective Daniels replies, "First, I'm sure the Silent Knight is a real person. I think he targets only criminals for a personal reason."

Detective Jackson nods, "Good assessment, but that's an easy conclusion. What else?"

Detective Daniels replies, "I think he is from San Francisco or has lived here for a long time because of his knowledge of the streets and how to avoid being seen."

Detective Jackson smiles and sits back, "I think we're going to work just fine together."

As they eat, they talk some more about their theories and once they are finished eating, they go to pay the check.

Detective Jackson speaks to his new partner as they walk out the door, "One thing I do know for sure is that it's going to get worse before it gets better."

DATE - August 26th, 1998
San Francisco, CA

Lisa Gellar, a reporter for the San Francisco Times and a beautiful 5'6" 130 pound young woman with blond hair and blue eyes appearing to be in her early to mid twenties, is sitting at the bar in one of the city's many strip clubs. Many men have noticed her given the fact that she is an attractive young woman dressed in a thigh length skirt and a tight fitting top. She has spent the last hour asking questions to the patrons to see if anyone has any information on the Silent Knight. So far, all she has managed to find out is how many drunk men want to take her home.

A big man in his early thirties walks up and sits next to her, "Hi, I'm Trace. Can I buy you a drink?"

Lisa smiles, trying to be polite, "I'm not drinking tonight."

The next dancer begins her routine and Trace speaks again, "So, what's your name?"

Lisa puts down her water, "Lisa."

Trace smiles, thinking he is getting somewhere, "So Lisa, do you want to go somewhere and get a bite to eat or something?"

Something about Trace makes Lisa uneasy, "No thanks."

Lisa gets up and decides to leave. Trace decides to follow her, not letting his drunken ego take no for an answer. Lisa walks to her car which is on the far side of the dark, poorly lit parking lot. As she unlocks the door, Trace grabs her from behind, wrapping his powerful right arm around her waist and placing his left hand over her mouth. Lisa tries to struggle, but Trace is just too strong. He drags her over to the other side of the parking lot where it is even darker. Trace uses his large body to pin Lisa up against a car. He pulls her skirt up and grabs the top of her underwear. Lisa continues to struggle, but the fear is keeping her from being able to scream for help.

Suddenly, Trace feels a hand grab the side of his neck and a terrible pain shoots through his body. Trace winces and his arms immediately let go of Lisa. Joseph reaches around Trace, grabs Lisa with his free hand and pulls Lisa away from Trace.

Joseph hears Kristen's voice, "Kill him Joseph. Make him suffer."

Joseph reaches around and grabs Trace's neck with his free hand. Joseph squeezes the throat until the windpipe collapses. Joseph lets go and Trace falls to the ground. As

Trace slowly suffocates, Lisa realizes she was just saved by the Silent Knight.

Lisa quickly digs through her purse for her camera. She pulls out the camera a few seconds later and looks back up. Silent Knight has vanished into the night and she is left alone with the dead body and a patch laying next to it.

DATE - August 29th, 1998
San Francisco, CA

Lisa Gellar is sitting at her desk, enjoying her first cup of coffee for the morning and looking through the messages on her desk. Some of her fellow workers have been razzing her about the story she wrote about her encounter with the Silent Knight. She flips to the next piece of paper in the stack of messages and her head drops a little. Lisa puts down the stack of messages and heads off for her boss' office.

Lisa walks into her boss' office knowing what this is going to be about, "You wanted to see me sir?"

Her boss, a man with graying hair in his fifties, tosses the paper on his desk with her story facing up, "What were you trying to do, get yourself killed?"

Lisa responds adamantly, "Everyone here is afraid to go after this Silent Knight story. I want it and I think I can break it."

Her boss speaks in an upset, but understanding tone, "What you did was careless. You didn't even think about all the bad things that could have happened to you, and almost did." Lisa stands quietly and her boss continues, "However, you're right, nobody else has even tried." He sighs, "This is probably a mistake, but I'm going to let you have the Silent Knight story. See what you can do with it, but be careful. No more reckless stunts."

Lisa smiles, "You got it."

Her boss nods to her and Lisa walks out of his office, thinking about what her next move will be.

DATE - September 13th, 1998
San Francisco, CA

As the sun starts to set, Joseph, wearing his vigilante outfit except for the mask and fedora, sits in front of the cross in the main room of the abandoned church. He has been thinking about Kristen all day. He contemplates ending his life in order to be with her again. Joseph looks down at the pistol in his right hand.

He hears Kristen's voice, "Hello Joseph."

Joseph looks right and sees Kristen standing a few feet away, "Kristen, is it really you?"

Kristen replies caringly, "Of course, I just wanted to let you know how proud I am of you."

Joseph gives her a sad smile, "Really, but wouldn't you be happier if we were together again?"

Kristen gives him an ever so loving smile, "Of course I would be, but your job on Earth isn't done yet. You have a chance to really make a difference. It's just not time for us to be together again."

Kristen's image slowly vanishes and Joseph looks back at the pistol and then up at the cross. He lets Kristen's words sink into his mind.

Joseph pictures Varges Martoni's face, "Kristen is right, I'm not done fighting yet."

DATE - September 21st, 1998
San Francisco, CA

Papa Martoni is in his kitchen preparing a dinner that has been passed down in his family for generations. One of his top men, the older gentleman that had suggested going after the Silent Knight, is in the kitchen with him. Suddenly, Papa Martoni drops the utensils and grabs his chest.

The older man looks at Papa Martoni, "Boss, are you okay?"

Papa Martoni is unable to answer as his left arm starts to go numb and he falls to the floor.

The older man yells, "Hey, someone help!"

In a matter of seconds, a younger man runs into the kitchen, "What's going on?"

The older man is kneeling next to Papa Martoni, "Something is wrong with the boss. Call 911."

The younger man runs off to make the call.

The older man looks back at Papa Martoni, "Hang in there boss, just hang in there."

The ambulance would arrive not long after the 911 call. Later that evening, Papa Martoni would be diagnosed as having his second heart attack.

That night, Varges would receive a call about his father. Varges wants so badly to return to San Francisco, but his father won't allow it. All because of this Silent Knight person.

DATE - October 31st, 1998
San Francisco, CA

On the cool, clear Halloween night, Josh Wilkinson, a young 5'9" 165 pound man of 17 years with short black hair and hazel eyes, stands on the edge of the roof of the twelve story downtown building. The building is closed for renovations so Josh figures he will not be bothered. Josh looks out over the city and thinks about what brought him to this decision.

Joseph is standing just twenty feet behind Josh, "Whatever brought you to this point, trust me, it's not worth it."

The voice startles Josh and he replies without looking back, "Leave me alone."

Joseph steps a little closer, still out of Josh's view, "Why would you want to do something like this?"

Josh sniffles as he thinks about the story behind his actions, "You wouldn't understand."

Joseph inches closer, still not giving away his identity, "Why don't you try me, what do you have to lose?"

Josh swallows hard, "I cared about her since we were kids. She is beautiful and popular so when she chose to go out with me, I was so excited. Until I found out it was a joke meant to embarrass me." A few tears run down his face, "I can't take it anymore. Everyone would be better off without me."

Joseph knows he has to get closer to this boy, "What's your name?"

Josh looks over and realizes who it is talking to him, "You're the Silent Knight. You're really ... real."

Joseph nods, knowing what the kid intends to do, "Yes I am, but you still didn't answer my question."

Josh replies shaking, "Josh." He pauses, "Are you going to kill me?"

Joseph smiles beneath his mask, "Why, have you committed a crime?" Joseph takes a step towards Josh and catches the kid off guard with his next question, "Do you still care about this girl?"

Josh looks down quietly for a second, "Yes I do." He looks back at Joseph, "But you don't understand. Have you ever felt like you didn't fit in? Have you ever had your heart broken?"

Joseph slightly nods as he steps closer, "Yes, to both. I even stood on this very same ledge before, then something occurred to me."

Josh looks at the vigilante, "What was that?"

Joseph takes a deep breath, "That no matter how bad things seem, it could always be worse. By ending it all, I would never know if things would have gotten better."

Josh starts to openly cry, "But I hurt so much."

Joseph speaks sympathetically, "Of course you do, that's how you know it's love. Look, you're young and so is she for that matter. Trust me when I say that there is someone out there for everyone. The future holds so many possibilities. Don't you want to be around to see things change?"

Josh shakes his head, "But I don't know if I could handle this kind of pain again."

Joseph offers a comforting voice, "Who says it will happen again? You never know what is going to happen. The only way to find out is to wake up tomorrow and start over again. I've started over many times in my life due to pain and hurt, but it has proven to me just how strong I am, and I know you're stronger than this." He pauses, "This girl might even be the right one for you, but it might not have been the right time. If you give up now, you will never know."

Josh can't help but think that the words make sense.

Josh starts to say something, "Maybe ..."

Josh stops and looks down to the street below.

Joseph takes another step closer, "If you've had any second thoughts, then it's not time for you to leave this

Earth." Joseph holds out his right hand, "Come on, I'll take you home."

Josh looks out over the city and then back at the Silent Knight, "Okay."

Josh takes the hand and Joseph leads the boy down to his motorcycle. Joseph takes Josh to a block away from his house. Josh gets off and starts to walk towards his house, then stops and turns around. The Silent Knight is gone, but Josh would never forget his words.

As far as Josh's future, six months later, the girl would apologize for the joke and the two of them would wind up falling in love and spending a long life together.

DATE - November 4th, 1998
San Francisco, CA

Joseph stands atop the watchtower in the park with his trench coat blowing in the cold night breeze. He watches as more and more people seem to be out and about than before he started his vigilante life. He has also seen more kids out playing during the day. Tonight he has seen three different couples walk through the park. He can't help but think that people are starting to feel more safe being out in the city and he can't help but feel like he is the reason.

He hears Kristen's voice, "You see Joseph, people do understand what you are doing."

Joseph looks over to his left to see Kristen standing there, "It all seems so unreal."

Kristen smiles, "It's real Joseph. You are making a difference in so many lives, but it's not over yet."

Joseph nods slightly, "Far from over."

Kristen's image vanishes, "I love you Joseph."

Joseph looks back out at the city and pictures the face of Varges Martoni. It still upsets him that Varges has disappeared, but tonight, he feels good about what he has accomplished in the time since he started and he smiles under his mask.

DATE - November 14th, 1998
San Francisco, CA

Gary Morris and Roger Mead, two men in their late sixties, have been getting together for twenty years at a coffee shop in their neighborhood for their morning coffee. Both of them have read the morning paper and the story about the Silent Knight.

Gary speaks, "So Roger, what do you think about the Silent Knight now?"

Roger shrugs ever the skeptic, "I'm still not sure. I don't think there is enough proof to say that a real vigilante is at work here. It could be the cops or the feds, or even a crime family covering up their work with this vigilante story."

Gary smiles having more of an open mind, "But people have claimed to see him."

Roger sits back, "They could have been paid to say those things. When dealing with the government or organized crime, you have to be careful about listening to what people say. Besides, it doesn't seem possible for one person to do all that this Silent Knight has done. I mean, how many has he killed?"

Gary puts down his coffee, "I think that the last count was 106." He pauses, "It would be interesting to know if he really exists."

The two men look back at the newspaper on the table and the Silent Knight story on the front page.

DATE - December 10th, 1998
San Francisco, CA

Well into the cold winter evening, Detective Daniels is sitting across from her partner at the station. The two detectives have been going over the latest case file on the Silent Knight.

Detective Jackson shakes his head, "There has to be a reason he targets only criminals, but what is it?"

Detective Daniels replies, "It's almost like." She pauses and gets a little excited, "Wait, that could be it."

Detective Jackson looks at her, "What's on your mind?"

Detective Daniels replies while shuffling through some photographs, "Revenge. That could be a good reason. Revenge against criminals for some wrong doing in his past."

Detective Jackson nods like why didn't he think of that, "We do have quite a few unsolved cases that might apply. If we go through them we might find a lead."

Detective Daniels stands up, "I'll start pulling the most violent unsolved cases."

Detective Jackson lets out a sigh, "I think we might be getting close."

Detective Daniels smiles at her partner and walks off while Detective Jackson continues to look through the papers on his desk.

DATE - December 23rd, 1998
San Francisco, CA

Joseph is sitting atop the watchtower in the park, looking out over the snow covered landscape. It has been dark for over an hour when Joseph sees a young couple, bundled up from the cold, come walking down one of the paths in the park towards the watchtower. He smiles to himself, but the smile quickly disappears when he sees a man approach the young couple.

Joseph watches as the man pulls a gun on the young couple. Joseph starts down the stairs as quickly as he can, hoping to get to the couple in time. As Joseph gets about twenty feet from the bottom of the stairs, he hears four loud gunshots. Joseph bursts out the door of the watchtower and starts running up the path towards the young couple. Joseph can see the two bodies laying in the blood covered snow and his anger rises.

Joseph stops by the bodies and looks around in the snow near the bodies. Joseph sees what he is looking for, a set of fresh tracks in the snow. He knows the tracks belong to the man responsible, and Joseph knows this will be as easy of a track as when he was a kid in Alaska. Joseph quietly follows the tracks for about three quarters of a mile and he sees the tracks disappear into a large group of bushes near the edge of the park. As Joseph approaches the bushes, he can hear movement from within the bushes.

Joseph moves into the bushes without a sound and sneaks right up behind the man who shot the young couple. Joseph kicks the man in the side of the head from behind. The man topples to the ground, dropping his gun in the snow. Joseph sees the pistol on the ground and he kicks it away into the bushes. The man staggers back to his feet and turns around. His glassy looking eyes can't believe who he is looking at.

The man manages two fearful words, "You're real."

Before the doped up man can move, Joseph kicks the man in the right leg, steps in and delivers a right elbow that shatters the man's nose. The kick and elbow are quickly followed by a left knee to the stomach. The man drops to his knees, gasping for air.

Joseph contemplates how to kill the man when he hears Kristen's voice, "Joseph, finish him slowly."

Joseph smiles beneath his mask and grabs the man's throat. Joseph locks eyes with the man as he slowly squeezes the life from the criminal. The man's body goes limp and Joseph lets it drop into the snow. Joseph drops his patch next to the body and disappears into the night.

Chapter 11

DATE - January 15th, 1999
San Francisco, CA

In the cold early morning, Joseph has been circling through the downtown area for the last two hours and all he has seen is the street people, hookers, nude and topless bars and the men that fancy that kind of entertainment. Joseph wonders what stories each of these men and women have for getting them into that kind of lifestyle. Joseph knows that some people wound up here because of things that were out of their control, but what he can't understand is why so many of the men that seek out that entertainment are married.

Joseph looks at his watch and considers heading for a different part of town when something catches his eye down one of the side streets. He sees a pimp yelling at a group of four girls that are dressed like they are in the business. He watches as the pimp pulls out a knife and cuts one of his girls across the face. The pimp then takes money from all four girls. Joseph takes off down the street towards the pimp, moving fast on his motorcycle.

The girls see the fast moving motorcycle and move out of the way. The pimp doesn't see the bike fast enough and

Joseph kicks the pimp with his right leg as he passes by. The pimp flies back against a parked car, then hits the ground hard. As Joseph slows down at the end of the block and turns his bike around, the pimp gets to his feet and pulls out his .38 caliber revolver.

The pimp fires twice and Joseph hears the bullets fly pass him. Joseph pulls his GLOC and returns a couple shots, but he too misses. With his heart pounding, the pimp fires two more shots, but this time he is not even close to hitting the vigilante. Joseph, as calm as can be, returns three more shots. The first one misses, the second hits the man in the right hip and the third hits the pimp in the sternum.

The pimp flies back against the parked car again, then he drops his pistol and slumps to the ground. This time the pimp doesn't get up as he slowly bleeds to death. Joseph rides up next to the body, drops his patch and takes off into the city streets.

DATE - February 6th, 1999
San Francisco, CA

In the early morning hours of the city, ten members of the Black Widow gang, a gang known for it's violence and recruiting of young kids, walk into an abandoned warehouse near Fisherman's Wharf with a young teenager. The huge open area, cluttered with barrels and various other items, is shrouded in darkness. One member walks over to the large power box, throws the switch and the darkness is lit up.

Joseph, who has been following the gang members for awhile, sneaks into the warehouse and quietly makes his way over to the power box. The gang initiation, which requires the new recruit to get a short beating by the other members, lasts only a couple minutes. Once the initiation is over, the gang starts to celebrate it's new member. Suddenly, the lights go out. In a panic, the gang scatters in the dark, each going a different direction.

Joseph slips up behind one gang member and quickly slit's the kid's throat with his combat knife. Not long after the first gang member goes down, another gang member hears something behind him. When the kid turns to see what it is, a throwing knife hits him in his chest. As Joseph retrieves his throwing knife, he hears two sets of footsteps heading for the main door.

Joseph comes up on two gang members heading for the door. Joseph kicks the legs out from under the kid on the right. The other kid quickly turns and manages to punch Joseph in the jaw. Joseph, obviously more skilled than the young gang member, spins with the punch and drops the kid with a spinning back fist. Joseph pulls out his pistol and kills the two kids with three shots.

Bullets come flying in Joseph's direction, but none come close as he can tell that the gang members are firing blind. Joseph fires his remaining three shots back into the darkness where he figures the shooting came from. His random shots wind up killing another gang member.

The remaining gang members run out of the ware-house and disappear into the streets. After searching through the warehouse for another five minutes, Joseph realizes the others must have gotten away.

Joseph sighs and speaks to himself, "We will meet again boys, you can count on it."

Joseph reloads his pistol, drops a patch and leaves the bodies for the police.

DATE - February 14th, 1999

San Francisco, CA

In the mid-morning hours of Valentine's Day, Joseph waits by the large oak tree near Kristen's grave until the cemetery is empty. Once he sees that the cemetery is empty, he walks over to Kristen's grave. Joseph is wearing his outfit except for his mask and gloves. He kneels and brushes some snow off the headstone. He places a candle on the headstone and lights it.

Joseph speaks to the headstone, "Well, it's been a year now. I miss you so much."

Kristen's voice, "You've done well Joseph."

Joseph looks left and sees Kristen standing a couple feet away, "I love you so much Kristen. I can't wait for the day we are together again."

Kristen smiles, "I love you Joseph and I too await that day."

Kristen's image vanishes and Joseph looks back at the headstone.

Kristen's voice again, "Remember, I can always see you and hear you. I pray for you every day."

Joseph smiles and he spends the next ten minutes thinking about his life with Kristen. Finally, Joseph turns to leave and he sees the caretaker looking at him from about two hundred feet away. Joseph just walks out of the cemetery.

DATE - February 26th, 1999

San Francisco, CA

After finishing her lunch, Lisa Gellar returns to her desk and starts going back over the recent stories of the Silent

Knight. Lisa is so wrapped up in her notes, she doesn't see Eileen Morgan walk up and sit down at the desk.

Eileen speaks, "How are you doing Lisa?"

Lisa looks up kind of startled, "Eileen." She pauses, "What are you doing here?"

Eileen smiles, "I just wanted to say hi."

Lisa sits back, "Why do I get the feeling that this is not a social call?"

Eileen sits forward, "Okay." Eileen gets a serious tone, "Look, alone we have turned up nothing on the Silent Knight. So, I thought that maybe we should start working together."

Lisa nods slightly still not completely convinced, "What did you have in mind?"

Eileen reaches into her bag and pulls out three note-books, "This is all the compiled information I've gathered on the Silent Knight. I figure that if we compile all our information together, we might be able to come up with some leads or ideas on who the Silent Knight is."

Lisa can tell that Eileen is sincere so she opens her desk and pulls out a couple notebooks, "That is not a bad idea."

The two reporters talk a little longer about how to approach the case. After agreeing on what the next step should be, they shake hands and get started on their work.

DATE - April 13th, 1999
San Francisco, CA

Detective Jackson and Detective Daniels are out patrolling the downtown streets around the midnight hour. Both detectives have noticed that the streets are busy with more regular citizens and fewer of what would be the criminal element.

Detective Jackson, who has been driving most of the night, sighs, "We have been driving around for hours. I don't know what we intend this to turn up."

Detective Daniels smiles from the passenger's seat, "You never know partner."

About that time, they see a motorcycle pull into an alley just down the street in front of them. Detective Jackson quickly pulls the car over and turns it off. The two detectives get out of the car.

Detective Jackson questions, "Do we really think this will be something?"

Detective Daniels starts walking towards the alley, "Have faith partner, we might just get lucky. We both know ..."

Her sentence is cut short as three gunshots ring out. The detectives draw their weapons and run as fast as they can for the alley. As the two detectives turn into the alley, they hear a motorcycle start up. Detective Jackson and Detective Daniels sprint down the alley. They stop when they come upon two dead bodies and a patch. The two detectives look up and see a person on a motorcycle about twenty five yards down the alley facing away from them.

Detective Daniels yells, "Police, don't move!"

Joseph turns on his bike and looks at the two detectives and sees their pistols aimed in on him. Both Detective Jackson and Detective Daniels gets a shocked look when they see the masked face, because they both know exactly who they are looking at. Joseph smiles beneath his mask because he can tell by the looks on the faces of the detectives that they won't shoot. Detective Jackson and Detective Daniels watch as the Silent Knight races off into the night, neither able to believe what just happened.

Detective Jackson looks at his partner with stunned disbelief, "It was him. He's real."

Detective Daniels is still a little shocked, "Yea, and we did nothing."

Detective Jackson shakes his head, "I forgot what to do. In all my years, this was the first." He pauses, "The first time I felt afraid of what could happen."

Detective Daniels lightly chuckles in agreement, "Me too."

Once the two detectives get their bearings back, they call in the encounter and begin to process the newest crime scene.

DATE - April 15th, 1999
San Francisco, CA

On a clear, cool day in the city, Detective Jackson and Detective Daniels are sitting at a table at a local restaurant, enjoying lunch. They have been discussing the night they saw the man himself, the Silent Knight.

Lisa Gellar walks in and over to the table where the detectives are sitting, "Detectives, I was wondering if I could ask you a few questions?"

Detective Jackson smiles knowing what Lisa is going to ask about, "About what?"

Lisa sits down, "About what you saw two nights ago." She smiles with anticipation, "Rumor has it, you two saw the Silent Knight with your own eyes."

Detective Daniels shakes her head, "We can't be exactly sure what we saw."

Lisa sighs knowing they are stalling, "Give me a break detectives. You two are the only law enforcement people that believe this guys exists. Let me help you change some minds."

Detective Jackson looks at his partner and Detective Daniels gives him a wink.

Detective Jackson lowers his voice, "Okay. We saw who we believe was the Silent Knight."

Lisa gets excited, "Did he look like others described? I can print a description for you."

Detective Daniels glances around and whispers, "Not yet. We don't want this guy to disappear or change his look. We need you to hold off a little longer, until we can find more clues to his identity."

Lisa nods, "You two are killing me, but okay, I guess I can wait. Just don't forget me when you break the case." She pauses, "Also, Eileen Morgan and I are working together to see if we might be able to find anything, so if there is anything we can help with, let us know."

Detective Jackson replies sarcastically, "I'm sure we will be in touch. Especially if Eileen is involved."

Lisa smiles and stands up, "Well, I'll leave you two to your food. Thanks detectives."

Lisa leaves and the detectives return to their lunch and theories.

DATE - April 20th, 1999
San Francisco, CA

Joseph waits in the shadows just outside the park restroom as the temperature drops the closer to midnight it gets. He watches the restroom intently.

As Joseph waits, he speaks to himself, "I can't believe the system would release a drug dealer and a child molester."

Joseph hears Kristen's voice, "You can't let these two get away. They will surely harm more kids if given the chance."

Joseph smiles beneath his mask, "They won't get away my love. They will never know what hit them."

As Joseph continues to wait, he thinks about the detectives that saw him. It was the first time anyone from law enforcement has actually seen him. Joseph knows that Detective Jackson is tenacious and seeing the Silent Knight will only make him more determined. Joseph didn't recognize the other detective.

About that time, the two men, both appearing to be in their forties, walk out of the restroom. Joseph quietly walks up behind them. The two men are completely unaware of the vigilante getting closer. The drug dealer screams out in pain as Joseph pulls his knife out of the man. Before the other man can move, Joseph kicks the child molester in the back of the legs, knocking him to the ground.

The child molester looks up at the Silent Knight with great fear in his eyes, "It's really you." He swallows hard and pleads, "But I've paid my debt to society."

Joseph shakes his head and speaks with great discontent for the man, "For what you did, there is only one punishment." He pulls out his pistol, "And that punishment is death."

Joseph puts four rounds into the child molester. Joseph holsters his pistol as both men bleed to death. Joseph drops his patch and disappears into the night.

DATE - May 19th, 1999
San Francisco, CA

Joseph has been sitting in the shadows of an alley that he knows is a place that has a lot of drug activity, especially when it's early morning. Joseph quietly watches a situation unfold as a plain clothes officer pushes a known drug dealer up against the wall.

The officer speaks kind of out of breath, "What do you think you're running from?"

The drug dealer replies, obviously winded, "Get off me. I wasn't running from nothing."

The officer smiles, "Oh really, lets have it. This month's payment."

The drug dealer eyes the officer, "Man, what if I decided to talk."

The officer looks seriously at the man, "Then I would kill you."

The drug dealer pauses, then smiles, "Man, I'm just joking. You need to lighten up."

Joseph watches as the drug dealer hands the officer a roll of cash and a small bag of cocaine. The scene sends a rage coursing through Joseph's veins. Joseph steps out of the shadows with his GLOC in his hand.

The drug dealer sees Joseph out of the corner of his eye, "No way!"

The officer draws his pistol and turns. The cop hurries his shot when he sees the vigilante and just misses Joseph. As the drug dealer runs off, Joseph fires twice, hitting the cop once in the left thigh. The officer falls to the ground and drops his pistol in front of him. As the officer reaches for his pistol, Joseph steps on the officer's wrist.

The officer looks up in obvious pain, "Kill me and you're through. Every cop in the city will be after you."

Joseph shakes his head and replies uncaringly, "My life ended when Kristen died, and every cop in the city is already looking for me." Joseph aims at the officer, "I guess this was not your night."

One shot rings out and the officer is dead. Joseph drops his patch and disappears into the night.

DATE - June 14th, 1999
San Francisco, CA

Detective Jackson and Detective Daniels are slowly driving through the park where the Silent Knight seems to operate the most from. It is evening time in the city and the sun has started to set. The two detectives are hoping for another chance encounter.

Detective Daniels looks at her partner, "It's probably too early."

Detective Jackson nods, "Probably so, but you never know."

Just then, they hear a scream and three shots ring out.

Detective Daniels gets excited, "This could be it."

Detective Jackson stops the car and puts it in park. The two of them get out and start towards the trees to their left. Suddenly, a motorcycle comes out of the trees, twenty yards to their right. As the motorcycle speeds away, Detective Daniels jumps in the driver's seat and Detective Jackson runs after the motorcycle to try and see if he can get a glimpse of anything to identify the bike with. Detective Daniels pulls up as they start to lose sight of the motorcycle and Detective Jackson jumps in the passenger's seat. They catch up to the motorcycle as it reaches the main road outside the park. Joseph glances in his mirror and sees the car. He makes out the two detectives and takes off like a bullet.

Detective Daniels switches on the lights, "He made us."

Detective Daniels' heart starts to pound as she floors the car and races after the Silent Knight.

Detective Jackson grabs the radio, trying to remain calm, "This is D671 in pursuit of suspect on an all black motorcycle that could be the Silent Knight. We are west bound on Chestnut Street just passing Larkin Street. Requesting backup."

The female dispatcher comes over the radio, "Copy. All units in the vicinity of Chestnut and Larkin. Join in pursuit of all black motorcycle with D671."

Joseph, staying as calm as possible, has put about half a block between him and the detectives, but Detective Daniels has managed to keep up. Joseph takes a quick left, but the car stays with him. Detective Jackson updates their location over the radio. Joseph speeds up to 55 mph and the car holds the distance. As the chase passes through the next intersection, two police cars fall in behind the detectives. Joseph fearlessly flies through a stoplight as cars swerve to miss him, but the pursuit holds it's distance.

Joseph takes a right, but the pursuit stays with him. Detective Jackson continues to update their location. Joseph jumps on one of the main highways that lead downtown as more police cars join in the chase. The police hold the distance to the speeding motorcycle and Detective Jackson updates their new location.

Detective Daniels speaks excitedly, "He's trying to get into downtown traffic."

Joseph speeds up to 90 mph and so does the police. Joseph slows down as he sees the highway blocked ahead of him. Joseph is forced to take the next exit which leads to the industrial park.

Detective Jackson speaks with excitement in his voice, "Okay, we should be able to corner him on one of the dead end streets."

Joseph opens up his bike some more, but the police stay on him and Detective Jackson radios the new location. The chase is heading towards numerous large business buildings.

Joseph sees another roadblock ahead so he quickly turns right. The police turn hard and fall behind. Then,

Joseph sees the road coming to a dead end and a huge building in front of him. Joseph slows down as he nears the end of the road.

Detective Daniels gets excited as she sees the end of the street, "We've got him."

Joseph rides up the stairs to the front of the building and spins his bike around. He sees all the cars coming down the street. Joseph knows the only way to lose them is to cut through the building, but he also knows that he will have to leave his motorcycle behind.

Detective Daniels and Detective Jackson watch as Joseph gets off his bike and runs for the building. Joseph smashes the glass door with his foot and runs inside the ten story building. The police pull up and jump out of their cars. With their hearts pounding, six police officers follow Detective Daniels into the building. Two police officers wait by the motorcycle. Detective Jackson knows the intentions of the vigilante so he looks for a way to get around the building.

Joseph gets to the back doors. The doors are metal and chained shut. He hears the police getting closer. Joseph looks right and sees the door to the stairs. He opens the stairwell door as Detective Daniels and the officers start down the hall towards him.

Detective Daniels yells as she runs, "He's in the stairwell."

Joseph has nearly reached the third floor as the police start up the stairs. Joseph gets to the tenth floor and opens the door. Detective Daniels looks up and sees the door to the tenth floor shut. The police gather themselves, then enter the tenth floor as Joseph disappears around a corner about two hundred feet away.

Detective Daniels barks out, "Be ready for anything." Joseph reaches the end of the long hallway which is a huge window. Joseph looks out the window. He sees a small parking lot, ten yards of grass and then a good sized pond. Joseph turns around and starts back down the hallway, looking for anyway to lose the police.

He gets about 75 feet from the window when the police come around the corner about 50 feet in front of him. Detective Daniels stops and the officers stop behind her. Joseph stops realizing he is trapped between the police and the window. He knows his only chance of escape as he turns, pulls out his pistol and runs for the window.

Detective Daniels screams, "Stop!"

Joseph shoots the window with five shots. He knows there is no turning back now. Detective Daniels watches in disbelief as the window shatters as Joseph jumps out of it. She is completely stunned by what she just saw. With his adrenaline running, Joseph flies out the window. It's an incredible jump as he lands in the middle of the pond with a huge splash.

Detective Daniels takes a second to collect herself, then runs over and looks out the window to see Joseph rush out of the water on the far side of the pond. She sees a tree line about fifty yards beyond the pond.

Detective Jackson comes around the side of the building and runs into a chain link fence. His heart drops as he watches Joseph disappear into the trees. Detective Jackson radios what just happened, but he knows it is too late. He knows that by the time the police make their way around to the other side of the industrial park, the Silent Knight will be long gone. Detective Jackson returns to the front of the building to wait for his partner.

DATE - July 2nd, 1999
San Francisco, CA

Detective Jackson and Detective Daniels are sitting at their desks enjoying the quiet of the early morning office while they go over the information on the motorcycle. Wanting to make sure she is the first to get any information, Eileen Morgan walks up.

Detective Jackson smiles at the reporter, "Eileen, to what do we owe this pleasure?"

Eileen returns the smile, "I'm happy to see you too detective." She gets to her usual inquisitiveness, "So, has the motorcycle given you any leads yet?"

Detective Daniels shakes her head, "We're still looking into it." She pauses and continues with some sarcasm, "Don't worry, we wouldn't keep you in the dark."

Eileen returns the sarcastic remark, "I'm sure you wouldn't." She turns back to Detective Jackson, "So, now that everyone knows the Silent Knight is real, what's the next move?"

Detective Jackson replies as if the answer is obvious, "Figure out who he is and catch him." Detective Jackson motions at his partner and they both stand up, "Now, if you'll excuse us, we have some work to do."

Eileen smiles, "Another time detective."

The two detectives walk off and Eileen leaves the police station.

DATE - July 16th, 1999
San Francisco, CA

Papa Martoni is sitting quietly in his den looking over the recent Silent Knight story in the paper. He wonders when and where it was that he lost control of the city.

Daniel walks in, "You wanted to see me?"

Papa Martoni looks up at Daniel, "Yes, please have a seat Dan."

Daniel sits, "What's on your mind Papa?"

Papa Martoni gets up, walks over to the window and stares at the setting sun for a moment, "So many things have changed. It's a whole new world out there." He pauses, "This Silent Knight has brought in a new era."

Daniel sits forward, "He won't be around forever. Either the police will catch him or someone will kill him."

Papa Martoni looks back at Daniel, "Do you know what an avenging angel is Dan?"

Daniel nods, "Yea."

Papa Martoni shakes his head, "The only person that can stop this Silent Knight is himself." He pauses again, "If something happens to me and Varges returns, I want the family to get away from it's criminal ways. I know Varges will want to go after this Silent Knight, but don't let him Daniel, don't let him."

Daniel nods, "I promise I'll do everything I can Papa."

Papa Martoni looks back out the window, "So many changes. Heed the lesson this Silent Knight has taught us. It's time to move on."

Daniel sits and quietly thinks about what was said while Papa Martoni continues to look out the window at the changing world.

DATE - August 3rd, 1999
Chicago, IL

In a beautiful mansion on the outskirts of Chicago, the early morning quiet is broken by a ringing telephone.

Vito Cicione, a distinguished looking man in his late fifties, answers the ringing phone, "Hello."

Daniel's voice, "Is Varges there?"

Vito speaks, "Who is this?"

Daniel's voice again, "It's Daniel Kelly. It's about his father."

Vito speaks again, "Just a minute."

A couple minutes later, Varges grabs the phone, "This is Varges, how are things going Dan?"

Daniel speaks solemnly, "I have some bad news Varges. I don't really know a good way to say this." He pauses for a second, "Varges, your father died late last night from a massive heart attack."

Varges is quiet for a few seconds, then replies with sadness in his voice, "Thanks for calling. I'll make arrangements for returning home."

The two friends talk for a couple more minutes, then hang up.

DATE - August 3rd, 1999
San Francisco, CA

Detective Jackson is sitting at his desk, enjoying his first cup of coffee for the day and his newspaper. He is waiting for his partner to show up. Detective Jackson looks up from his newspaper to see Detective Daniels walking up.

Detective Jackson smiles at her, "Sleeping in are we?"

Detective Daniels sits down at her desk, "Guess what I heard?"

Detective Jackson looks at her, "What is it?"

Detective Daniels sits back in her chair, "Papa Martoni died of a heart attack late last night."

Detective Jackson shakes his head, "You're kidding me. There is nothing in the paper about it."

Detective Daniels smiles, "I have a friend that works at the hospital and was there when it happened."

Detective Jackson has a look of disbelief, "Unbelievable, I guess this means his son will take over the business."

Detective Daniels gets a puzzled look, "His son?"

Detective Jackson puts down his coffee, "Yea. His son, Varges Martoni."

Detective Daniels replies, "I don't think I know his son."

Detective Jackson explains, "Varges disappeared after walking free from his murder trial, but I'm sure he will be back now that his father has died." He picks up a file from his desk, "Well, shall we see what the lab has for us on the motorcycle."

Excited to see what the crime lab has found out about the motorcycle, Detective Daniels doesn't catch what her partner just said about Varges walking free from murder.

Chapter 12

DATE - August 6th, 1999
San Francisco, CA

Joseph, wearing his vigilante clothes without the trench coat, mask, gloves and fedora, sits in front of the cross in the main room of the abandoned church. Joseph drops the old newspaper. His face has a look of disbelief at what he just read. Papa Martoni is dead and Varges is gone. He feels lost and confused about who he has to exact his revenge on now. Plus, Papa Martoni was probably his only link to Varges.

Joseph looks up at the cross, "With both of them gone, what's the point of going on?"

Kristen's soothing voice, "You must keep your faith Joseph."

Joseph looks to his right and sees Kristen standing a few feet away, "What's the point of continuing Kristen? Varges is gone and Papa Martoni was probably the only person who knew how to find him."

Kristen moves closer and reassures him, "Things will work out Joseph, you just have to keep up the hope." She takes on a serious tone, "You're not through teaching these people their lesson."

Joseph smiles, feeling a little better, "You always have a way of knowing what to say."

Kristen gives a loving smile, "I love you Joseph, always remember that."

Joseph replies as her image fades, "I love you too."

Joseph is alone once again and for the first time since his parents and sister died, Joseph kneels in front of the cross and says a prayer.

DATE - September 2nd, 1999
San Francisco, CA

Detective Jackson and Detective Daniels are sitting at their desks as their work has carried them into the after dinner hours. They just finished going over the last plausible lead from their unsolved cases.

Detective Jackson sits back in his chair, "Nothing. Can you believe it? Nothing that seems to fit with the Silent Knight."

Detective Daniels closes the last file, "I can't believe how something like this can just fall through the cracks. You think the system would work better."

Detective Jackson looks up like something shocked him, "That's it! What if ..." His mind locks on what he said about Varges Martoni, "What if the case was solved, but failed in court?"

Detective Daniels nods, "Those files would be in the unsolved cases room, but in a different section." She gets a little excited, "But if that happened to me, I would sure want some revenge."

Detective Jackson nods in agreement, "So would I."

Detective Daniels stands up, "I'll go and start pulling the files."

Detective Jackson nods and picks up his phone, "I'll be there in a minute."

He dials a number that he knows all too well and Eileen Morgan answers, "Hello."

Detective Jackson speaks, "Eileen, I need your help."

Eileen recognizes the voice right away, "What can I do for you detective?"

Detective Jackson replies, "Can you get me a list of any big or unusual news that occurred from September of 1997 to March of 1998?"

Eileen replies in her usual reporter tone, "You are onto something, aren't you?"

Detective Jackson replies, "We might be. Can you do that for me?"

Eileen replies with an of course I can attitude, "No problem. I can get it to you in a few days."

Detective Jackson sounds a little happier, "Thanks. I owe you one."

Eileen chuckles lightly, "Boy do you detective. I'll see you in a couple of days."

The two of them hang up. Detective Jackson goes off to help his partner pull files, while Eileen gets on her computer and starts to gather the information for Detective Jackson.

DATE - September 5th, 1999
San Francisco, CA

As the sun starts to rise, Eileen Morgan and Lisa Gellar walk into the police department. Eileen is carrying a three inch binder full of papers and Lisa is carrying four large coffees from McDonalds. Eileen and Lisa walk over to the desks of the two detectives and sit down.

Eileen puts the binder on Detective Jackson's desk, "I figured with this much paper to go through, we would need some coffee." She pauses, "Oh, by the way, in case you didn't know, this is Lisa Gellar, we are working together on the Silent Knight story."

Lisa nods to the two detectives and Eileen continues, "The biggest thing to happen during the time you asked was the Varges Martoni trial."

Detective Jackson nods, "I think we should start with the Martoni family and all the possible leads from the trial." He pauses, "Wasn't there a guy during the trial, the witness, he was extremely upset over the outcome."

Lisa nods, "Yes, Kristen Shobe's future husband, Joseph Thompson. His car was pulled out of the bay not long after the trial."

Detective Daniels sighs, "Well, we won't start there then. Lets see what else we have."

The four of them start going through the list of possibilities and matching them up with police files. Each person has butterflies building in their stomachs as they feel they are getting closer to cracking the Silent Knight case.

DATE - September 28th, 1999
San Francisco, CA

As the afternoon drizzle lets up, giving way to the sun, a black limo pulls up to the Martoni home. Two men in suits get out of the back, then Varges Martoni steps out. The driver pulls Varges' bags out of the back as Daniel walks up to the car.

Varges smiles, "It's good to be home again." He nods to Daniel, "Hello Dan. It's good to see you again."

The two old friends shake hands as the other two men grab Varges' bags.

Varges speaks to Daniel as they walk towards the house, "We need to start building back up right away. Plus, we definitely need to handle this Silent Knight problem."

Daniel shakes his head, "I don't know Varges. Your father avoided the Silent Knight. He even considered taking the family out of the business all together."

Varges chuckles slightly, "Yea, right."

Daniel stops and looks at Varges, "I'm serious Varges. Your father actually said that the Silent Knight scared him. He called him an avenging angel."

Varges stops, "Huh, I never heard of my father talking like that about anyone." Varges slowly nods his head, "I'll address the men once I get settled in."

Daniel nods and the two men continue into the house.

DATE - October 3rd, 1999

San Francisco, CA

Joseph sits on the ledge of the building where he helped Josh all those months ago. He looks out over the city enjoying the fall night and he can't believe what he is seeing.

Joseph smiles beneath his mask, "Kristen, there are so many people out tonight. It's amazing."

He hears Kristen's voice, "You've made the city a safer place. People know that there is someone out there protecting them."

Joseph nods to himself, "You're right Kristen, it is a safer place now."

Kristen's soothing voice replies, "And now only one thing remains."

Joseph takes on a more serious tone, "Varges Martoni."

Kristen's voice slowly fades, "Yes, and his time is coming. It's coming soon."

Joseph sighs as the images of the night he lost Kristen flash through his mind. He does his best to push the horrible images from his mind and replace them with images of all the fun times he and Kristen had together. He also tries to focus on all the good he has done since becoming the Silent Knight.

Joseph closes his eyes and listens to the city. In all the crazy noise, Joseph can hear it in his mind, he can hear the city thanking him for everything that he has done.

DATE - October 14th, 1999

San Francisco, CA

Detective Daniels is on her way home after a long day of work. She looks at her watch and notices that it is nearly midnight. She looks around, wondering where the Silent Knight might be. She sees a convenience store up ahead and decides to stop. She pulls into a parking spot next to an empty car that still has it's motor running.

Detective Daniels gets out of her car. As soon as she closes her door, three masked men come out of the front door of the store. One man has an AK-47 and the other two have shotguns.

Instinctively, Detective Daniels draws her pistol as her heart starts beating faster, "Freeze, police!"

As the three men turn to her, Detective Daniels fires a reign of bullets while backing up towards the trunk of her car. She stops firing and ducks behind the rear of her car for cover. Her numerous bullets hits one of the men with a shotgun and that man falls as the other two open fire. The car shakes violently as it takes incredible punishment. Knowing she is well out-gunned, Detective Daniels reloads, pops up and fires again. She drops back down as the men fire back.

Detective Daniels comes back up and fires the rest of the clip in her pistol as the men hide behind the front of her car and return fire. She reloads with her last clip as the men reload. She can hear sirens in the distance, but she can tell that the backup will never arrive in time. She comes up shooting again, but misses. The man with the shotgun starts down the passenger's side of the car as the man with the AK-47 starts down the driver's side. Detective Daniels comes up firing and kills the man with the shotgun with her last four shots. She drops back down and looks at her empty pistol.

Suddenly, the man with the AK-47 steps around the back of the car and looks at Detective Daniels. The two of them lock eyes and given the intensity of the gun battle, they are completely unaware of their surroundings. Detective Daniels takes a deep breath and closes her eyes, knowing she is about to die.

Detective Daniels hears a single shot echo in the night. She opens her eyes to see the man with the AK-47 laying dead, a single shot to the head. She stands up in time to see the Silent Knight drop a patch and ride off on his new bike.

Detective Daniels can't believe that the Silent Knight just saved her life. Then she gets a cold chill down her spine as she thinks, what if the Silent Knight didn't exist.

DATE - October 17th, 1999
San Francisco, CA

Lisa Gellar is waiting in her car on the police station parking lot. She is waiting for Detective Daniels to show up for work. Lisa waits another ten minutes, then Detective Daniels pulls in and parks her car. Lisa gets out of her car.

Lisa walks over to Detective Daniels as she gets out of her car, "Detective Daniels, I was wondering if you had any comment about the other night?"

Detective Daniels replies, "No, not really."

Detective Daniels starts to walk off and Lisa follows her, "The Silent Knight saved your life, didn't he?"

Detective Daniels stops and turns to Lisa, "What makes you say that?"

Lisa glances around to make sure they are alone, "I saw the crime scene. That's the only possibility I can come up with."

Detective Daniels turns and walks off, "Yes he did."

Lisa shouts, "How do you feel about that?"

Detective Daniels keeps on walking. She leaves the question unanswered, because she really doesn't know how to answer it since her feelings have started to change about the Silent Knight.

DATE - November 30th, 1999
San Francisco, CA

Joseph watches from the shadows of the cold night as two Martoni men, one that appears to be in his late twenties and one that appears to be in his forties, walk across the parking lot of a restaurant after an excellent dinner. Joseph looks around and sees that no one else is on the parking lot. He slowly moves towards the two men.

The younger man speaks, "I can't wait to see what Varges does about this Silent Knight."

The older man nods, "I know. I loved Papa Martoni, but Varges will get us back in control of San Francisco."

As the two men near their car, the younger man walks around to the driver's side and the older man walks over to the passenger's side. The younger man looks down and unlocks the driver's door. When the younger man looks back up, a shocked look comes to his face as he sees the barrel of a GLOC pointed over the roof of the car at him.

Joseph is standing right behind the older man. He has his combat knife in his left hand and it is pressed against the older man's throat and he has his pistol in his right hand pointed at the younger man. In one quick motion, Joseph cuts the older man's throat the same time he puts two bullets into the younger man. Joseph steps back from the car as both men lay bleeding on the pavement. Joseph smiles beneath his mask as he has heard everything the two men have said about Varges. He puts his weapons away, drops his patch and walks off.

DATE - December 15th, 1999
San Francisco, CA

Joseph sits in his special place, the place where he took Kristen fishing. He takes in the brisk morning air as he watches the sun rise. He has been feeling good the last couple of weeks since hearing that Varges Martoni is back in San Francisco.

Joseph hears Kristen's voice, "I told you things would work out."

Joseph looks left at Kristen and smiles, "I was hoping you would be here. I guess you know about Varges."

Kristen nods, "Yes. Now you can finish it. Now you can make things right."

Joseph nods slightly, "I will make things right again. I will teach Varges the ultimate lesson."

Kristen shows a loving smile, "I love you Joseph. It's getting closer to the time for us to be together again."

Joseph returns the loving smile, "I can't wait for that day. I love you very much."

Kristen's image fades away and Joseph is alone again. He takes a little walk, replaying days of old with Kristen.

DATE - December 30th, 1999
San Francisco, CA

Joseph is sitting in the main room of the abandoned church. He looks over the miniature he made of the Martoni landscape. He goes over all the different possible ways to approach the well protected house. He knows Varges will have some men staying with him. He also knows that he will have to improvise once inside the house since he has never been in the Martoni home.

Joseph spends a couple more hours going over every option and what to do if something goes wrong. More importantly, he goes over his plan on what to do once Varges is dead. He knows it is only a matter of time before Detective Jackson figures out who he is.

DATE - January 13th, 2000
San Francisco, CA

Detective Jackson and Detective Daniels continue their late night vigil as they look through Eileen's list and the case files. Detective Jackson notices a clipping from a newspaper. The clipping reads: "Joseph Thompson's Body Not Found In Car".

Detective Jackson slams his hands on his desk, "That's it! That has to be it!"

Detective Daniels looks up in surprise, "What did you find?"

Detective Jackson looks at his partner, "Do you remember what Varges Martoni was on trial for?"

Detective Daniels nods, "He was on trial for the murder of Kristen Shobe."

Detective Jackson nods, "Right, and the witness was her future husband, Joseph Thompson."

Detective Daniels shrugs, "So, his car was pulled out of the bay soon after the trial."

Detective Jackson hands the clipping to his partner, "Yes, his car was, but his body was never found."

Detective Daniels looks at the clipping, "He staged his own death."

Detective Jackson sits back, "Exactly, he did it so he could get his revenge on Varges Martoni. I remember vividly how upset he was over the verdict and he said something about never stop fighting. It just ..." He sighs, "It has to be him."

Detective Daniels sits forward, "You said Varges disappeared soon after the trial."

Detective Jackson nods, "He did, but now he is back in San Francisco." He smiles, "Ten to one, Joseph Thompson is the Silent Knight. Twenty to one, Varges Martoni is his next target."

Detective Daniels smiles at her partner, "Good work, detective."

DATE - January 31st, 2000
San Francisco, CA

The sun starts to set over the city as Detective Daniels and Detective Jackson gets comfortable in their car outside the

Martoni home as their stakeout shift has just begun. Detective Daniels and Detective Jackson watch on as Varges Martoni gets out of a limo and walks into his house.

Detective Daniels sighs, "It's been nearly three weeks and not a single sign of the Silent Knight." She looks over at her partner, "You don't think he recognized us do you?"

Detective Jackson replies casually, "As much as he hates Varges Martoni, I don't think it would matter. He's coming for him, with or without us here."

Detective Daniels speaks, "You know what, just between us, I'm not sure I want to keep the Silent Knight from killing Varges Martoni."

Detective Jackson looks at his partner, "Your attitude has seemed different since the night he saved your life."

Detective Daniels sighs, "I have gone over that night so many times in my head. If the Silent Knight didn't exist, I wouldn't be sitting here."

Detective Jackson nods slightly, "You can't dwell on it." He pauses, "When you think about it, you might not have ever been in that situation if the Silent Knight didn't exist."

Detective Daniels smiles as she finds her partner's attempts to be psychological kind of funny, "I know, but the fact remains, he saved my life." She pauses, "And he is doing all of this for the love of a woman. Varges is a bad man. I just don't know if I want to stop the Silent Knight from killing him."

Detective Jackson looks at his partner, "You know what?" She looks at him and Detective Jackson continues, "I feel the same way."

Detective Daniels smiles at her partner. The two detectives continue to watch the house until their replacements arrive.

DATE - February 13th, 2000

San Francisco, CA

Joseph is kneeling in front of the cross in the main room of the abandoned church. He finishes saying his prayer. He looks at his watch and it shows 10:45 pm.

Joseph speaks to himself, "By this time tomorrow, it will all be over and Varges will be dead.", Joseph looks back up at the cross, "Soon Kristen, it will be finished. I'll be with you again, soon."

Joseph gears up, gets on his motorcycle and heads for the Martoni home.

DATE - February 14th, 2000

San Francisco, CA

In the darkness of the early morning hour, Joseph parks his motorcycle about half a mile from the back wall of the Martoni home. Joseph recognized the two detectives watching the front of the house. He knows that they must have figured him out. Joseph knew it would only be a matter of time. Joseph makes his way up to the back wall surrounding the land. He quickly scales it and lands quietly on the other side. He makes his way up to the back of the house and so far he has not seen anyone.

Joseph jimmies open a window, figuring that he will set off a silent alarm, and climbs into the house. Joseph finds himself in the kitchen. He looks for and finds the fuse box in the laundry room just off the kitchen. Most of the lights are off in the house, but he can hear the television in the background. Joseph takes a deep breath and knows it's now or never. He shuts off all the power to the house.

Varges is laying in bed watching television when the lights go out. He gets up, gets dressed in jeans, a t-shirt and tennis shoes and grabs his pistol from the nightstand. Varges walks over to his bedroom window. He can see the lights that line the wall are still on. Varges knows it can only be one thing, the Silent Knight has come.

Daniel and Jacob, the two men staying with Varges, are watching television in the living room when the power goes out. The two men get up from their seats and draw their pistols. Jacob, a stout young man in his early twenties wearing a collared shirt and Dockers, heads for the dining room and Daniel, wearing jeans and a t-shirt, starts for the kitchen.

Detective Jackson and Detective Daniels watches the power to the house go out. They look around and see that the house lights are the only lights out. The two detectives draw their weapons, get out of their car and slowly start towards the front gate.

Joseph quietly makes his way into the dining room. He hears someone coming his way so he draws his knife and waits in the dark. Jacob cautiously enters the dining room and starts around the large dining table. Jacob is sure that if anyone is in the room, they will be able to hear his heart pounding. Then, out of the darkness, Joseph grabs Jacob's gun hand and breaks the wrist with a sharp twist. Joseph drives the knife into Jacob's neck. Jacob is unable to make a loud enough sound for anyone to hear. Joseph slowly and quietly lowers Jacob's body to the floor.

Joseph makes his way into the main hall and stands at the bottom of the stairs. The main hall is about fifty feet wide with some furniture lining the walls. The moonlight shines through the windows, providing some light. Joseph puts his knife away as Daniel steps into the main hall across from Joseph. Joseph moves for cover and Daniel sees the movement. Daniel, in a nervous rush, fires into the dark.

Varges hears the shot and knows it is time to face the Silent Knight. Daniel takes a couple of steps forward and he is hit in the chest by a throwing knife. Daniel cries out and falls to the floor. Varges realizes that Jacob and Daniel are probably dead and he is now alone. Showing no fear, he heads out of the bedroom for the stairs.

Detective Jackson heads back to the car as Detective Daniels waits by the gate.

Varges slowly walks down the stairs and he sees Daniel's lifeless body. When Varges reaches the bottom of the steps, Joseph lunges out and grabs his wrist holding the pistol. Joseph twists the arm around and slaps the pistol out of Varges' hand. Joseph does a quarter spin and throws Varges to the floor. Varges scrambles to his feet and turns to face the vigilante.

Joseph speaks coldly, "It ends tonight."

Varges replies confidently, "It ends for you."

Varges throws a quick left hook at Joseph. Joseph catches the arm, twists around and throws Varges into the nearby china cabinet. The glass and porcelain dishes shatter as Varges falls to the floor with a few cuts on his arms and hands.

Joseph speaks without emotion, "You're going to feel a lot of pain before I kill you."

Varges gets up and rushes Joseph. Joseph steps to the side, grabs Varges and throws him to the floor again. As Varges starts to stand, Joseph kicks him in the chest. Varges falls to the floor again and lets out a grunt of pain. Joseph stands patiently and waits for Varges to get back on his feet.

Joseph steps towards Varges, "You're going to pay for what you did to Kristen."

Varges shakes his head, "I don't think so."

Varges feints a punch and kicks Joseph in the stomach with a straight kick. Joseph takes a few steps back, never losing his balance.

Varges chuckles, "Yea, how about that?"

Joseph smiles beneath his mask, "If that is the best you got, you should have never come back."

Varges feints a kick this time and hits Joseph with a right hook. Joseph spins with the punch and his right leg drops Varges with a spin kick.

Joseph takes a step at Varges, "It's time to die."

Varges gets up and throws another quick left hook. Joseph blocks with his right arm and wraps his arm around Varges' left arm. Joseph quickly snaps Varges' left elbow. Joseph follows by quickly cutting Varges' left knee with his right foot. As Varges goes down, Joseph comes around and delivers a knee to Varges' nose, shattering it. Blood flies everywhere as Varges falls to his back. Joseph steps back and slowly pulls out his pistol.

Varges looks up at the masked vigilante, knowing he is going to die, "Only a coward kills behind a mask."

Joseph throws his hat to the floor and pulls off his mask.

Joseph drops the mask, "I told you before that the fight wasn't over, that you never stop fighting until the fight is done."

The first sign of fear comes to Varges' face as he re-members the time he heard those words, the trial for Kristen Shobe. Varges looks at the man who has waited for two years to have his revenge.

Joseph aims his pistol and speaks with all the hatred in his soul, "This lesson is over."

A shot rings out and Varges is dead. Joseph holsters his pistol and drops a patch. He leaves his fedora and mask on the floor and heads for the back.

Detective Jackson crashes his car through the gate and the two detectives rush to the house. Detective Jackson kicks in the front door and Detective Daniels rushes in to see the carnage left by the Silent Knight. The two detectives put their weapons away, knowing that they are too late. Detective Jackson sees a patch laying next to the mask and hat. Detective Daniels calls for backup and once it arrives and the crime scene processed, they head for the station.

Once back at the station, the two tired detectives sit at their desks. Detective Daniels looks at her watch to see that it is nearly six in the morning.

Detective Daniels rubs her eyes, "I can't believe he got away."

Detective Jackson sees the date on the calendar, "Happy Valentine's Day partner."

Detective Daniels quickly sits up and looks at him, "Wait a minute. Today is February 14th?"

Detective Jackson nods, "Yea, why?"

Detective Daniels starts shuffling through papers, "I've seen that date before in the file. When did Kristen Shobe die?"

Detective Jackson can tell his partner is onto something, "It was September 28th."

Detective Daniels grabs the paper about Kristen Shobe, "Kristen Shobe was born on February 14th."

Detective Jackson nods, "I bet he went to her grave."

Detective Daniels smiles, "She is buried at the Parkview Cemetery."

The two detectives get up and head for the cemetery. They both know it is a long shot, but they have to check it out. Joseph is standing at Kristen's grave. The sun has started to rise. He has on everything except the mask and hat. Joseph places a candle on the headstone and lights it.

A few minutes later he hears a car pull up followed by two doors opening and closing. Joseph smiles as the two detectives walk up behind him with their hands on their guns.

Joseph speaks without turning around, "I've been waiting for you two. I knew you would figure it out."

Detective Jackson removes his hand from his pistol, "You're Joseph Thompson, right?"

Joseph nods slightly, "Yes I am."

Detective Daniels notices the burning candle, "What's the candle for?"

Joseph looks at her, not expecting that question, "It's a promise I made to Kristen as she died in my arms, eternal flame for eternal love."

Detective Jackson questions, "Is it over now Joseph?"

Joseph nods, "It's over, Kristen is happy now." Joseph looks down at the candle, "I love you Kristen."

Joseph hands over his weapons and allows himself to be handcuffed. Detective Jackson puts him in the back of the car and the three of them head for the station. As they make their way through the city streets, the three of them know that the Silent Knight is over, but they also know that the legend has only begun.

Chapter 13

DATE - February 15th, 2000
San Francisco, CA

In the morning hours of the day, numerous citizens of San Francisco sit down to watch the news, four of which are Mr. and Mrs. Lee and William and Becky Shobe.

Eileen comes on the air in front of the police station, "Good morning San Francisco, we have breaking news in the Silent Knight story. At about 2 am yesterday morning, Varges Martoni was allegedly killed by the Silent Knight. Sources within the police department say that the Silent Knight later turned himself in to Detective Darius Jackson and Detective Pamela Daniels."

The news shocks everyone who hears it, but nothing would be more surprising than what comes next.

Eileen continues, "The Silent Knight's true identity is believed to be Joseph W. Thompson, originally from Alaska, but raised here in San Francisco. The trial is set to start on March 1st. We will bring you more of this breaking story as we get the information. Have a good morning San Francisco."

The Lees and Shobes are shocked at the news. The news that Joseph is still alive.

DATE - March 1st, 2000
San Francisco, CA

In the mid-morning hours of the spring like day, Detective Jackson and Detective Daniels are waiting by their car for the jailors to bring Joseph to them. The two detectives hear the large steel door to the jail buzz, then open. A male jailor comes through the door first. Joseph comes through the door next and he has on an orange jumpsuit, belly chains and leg shackles. The last one out the door is a female jailor and she is carrying some papers in her left hand.

Detective Jackson and Detective Daniels takes control of Joseph from the jailors. Detective Daniels puts Joseph in the backseat as Detective Jackson takes the paperwork from the female jailor. The jailors walk back into the jail. Detective Jackson gets in behind the wheel and Detective Daniels gets in next to Joseph.

They pull out of the police station and head for the courthouse with another police car right behind them. People are all over the streets holding signs of support for Joseph, thanking him for all the things he has done. Both detectives look around in amazement as neither one can believe the number of people and even Joseph is looking around in surprise. The cars pass a playground and all the kids start waving and cheering.

Detective Daniels looks out the window, "Look at all those people you affected."

Joseph smiles at all the support, "Someone had to take a stand. I excelled where the system failed. I fought the fights others dared not to."

Detective Jackson looks at Joseph in the rearview mirror, "Was it worth it?"

Joseph nods slightly, "Yes it was. It was what Kristen wanted."

The mile and a half drive is slow with all the people in the streets. Finally, the two cars pull into the parking lot of the courthouse. Detective Jackson parks the car and gets out. He waits until the other two police officers and the two armed courtroom guards are next to the car, then he opens the back door and Joseph and Detective Daniels gets out. The armed guards take the paperwork from Detective Jackson and take control of Joseph.

Detective Daniels decides that she has to say something as they take Joseph away, "Thank you, for saving my life."

Joseph looks back at her, "You are very welcome."

The guards take Joseph into the courthouse for the beginning of his trial.

DATE - April 27th, 2000
San Francisco, CA

Joseph has finished his lunch and he lays down on his bunk in his small isolation cell.

A female jailor walks up to the door of the cell, "Thompson, you have visitors. Get ready."

Joseph puts on his jumpsuit and shower shoes. Once dressed, the female jailor opens the cell door. The female jailor escorts Joseph from his cell to the visitor's room. Joseph walks in and sees Mr. Lee, Mrs. Lee, William and Becky sitting at a table. Joseph walks over and sits across from them.

William speaks with happiness, "It's good to see you again Joe."

Becky has tears in her eyes, "I'm so happy you're alive. Are you okay?"

Joseph nods slightly, "I'm fine." He takes an apologetic tone, "I'm sorry for putting you all through this. It was something I had to do."

Mrs. Lee tries to hold back the tears, "We are just happy to see you again. We know you had your reasons for doing what you did."

Joseph sighs, "I had to make things right." He pauses and looks at Mr. Lee, "Father, I bet you're disappointed in me for using my training to kill others."

Mr. Lee shakes his head reassuringly, "No. I could not be more proud of you, my son. You used your training to help make the world a better place and that is all I could ask of you." He pauses and smiles, "Enough about that, we have a lot of catching up to do."

The five of them visit for the thirty minutes. They talk about the old times. When the half hour is over, the female jailor escorts Joseph back to his cell. Joseph lays down on his bunk and stares up at the ceiling in his cell. He feels better having his family back, but he still feels the over-whelming emptiness of Kristen being gone.

DATE - May 14th, 2000
San Francisco, CA

Lisa Gellar is sitting at her desk putting the finishing touches on her story about the trial so far.

Lisa's boss walks up to her, "So, how did it go today?"

Lisa looks up at her boss, "It went pretty much as planned. Just one unexpected thing."

The boss gets a puzzled look, "What is that?"

Lisa sits back, "The defense lawyer didn't even ask me a question. That, plus when the trial started, the defense made a motion to put off it's opening statement until the prosecution is done making it's case." She pauses, "I don't know, it's just driving me crazy, because I've never seen anything like this before."

Her boss nods, "I don't know about not asking questions, but as far as the opening statement, I've seen it done once, and it worked. The opening statement can leave a powerful affect on the jury."

Lisa nods, "Yea." She pauses, "I don't know, it's like the defense is not wanting to win the case."

Her boss smiles at her, "The legal system is crazy and with lawyers, you never know what to expect." He pauses for a second, "Well, I'll let you get back to your story. If you need anything, just let me know."

Lisa nods and her boss walks off. She thinks about her testimony and the fact that the defense lawyer never asked her a question. She puts it out of her mind and gets back to her work. Once her copy is done, she takes the story down to the editing office.

DATE - June 12th, 2000
San Francisco, CA

In the warmth of the summer afternoon, Eileen Morgan stands outside the courthouse as the trial ends for the day. This is a place she has found herself at every day since the trial began. She watches over the crowd as citizens and law enforcement makes their way down the front steps. Then, Eileen sees the DA, an average sized African-American man in his mid-forties wearing a dark blue suit, walk out of the building.

Eileen walks over to the DA, "Excuse me Mr. Dawson, I was wondering how you felt it went today?"

Mr. Dawson stops, "All I can say is that the case is airtight. That fact along with the fact that the defense doesn't seem interested in defending themselves, I feel a conviction is in Joseph Thompson's future. Now, if you will excuse me, I must go."

Mr. Dawson walks off. Eileen interviews a couple law enforcement officers, then calls it a day.

DATE - July 15th, 2000
San Francisco, CA

Joseph's lawyer, a distinguished looking man in his early fifties, walks into Mr. Dawson's office.

Mr. Dawson greets the defense lawyer, "Mr. Reid, please have a seat."

Mr. Reid takes a seat, "What's on your mind Mr. Dawson?"

Mr. Dawson sits, "I was wondering about your defense. Are you going to defend your client?" He pauses, "I would hate to see Mr. Thompson file an appeal because of his legal help."

Mr. Reid smiles, "Not that I am use to sharing my strategy with the state before I make my case." He pauses for a second, "But Mr. Thompson's actions over the last two years defend him."

Mr. Dawson sits forward with a puzzled look, "What are you talking about?"

Mr. Reid responds, "We had this case won the day we walked into the courtroom for the first time." He smiles, "Do you really think you can find a citizen out there that will convict my client for what he did and especially, why he did it? I think not."

Mr. Dawson gives a slight nod, "I see your point, but you should be more careful. The people can be very unpredictable. A person can surprise you." He pauses, "Even

I respect what your client did, but the law is the law. Just so you know, I will entertain a plea bargain."

Mr. Reid stands, "Mr. Thompson has made it clear that I am not to discuss any kind of plea agreement. He has it in his own mind how this trial is going to go and I work for him. I guess we will see how it goes. It was nice talking to you."

Mr. Reid leaves the office. The DA sits back and wonders if he can make a good enough case to get a conviction, and does he really want to.

DATE - August 21st, 2000
San Francisco, CA

Once the trial ends for the day, Detective Daniels walks out of the courthouse. She has been having mixed emotions over helping put Joseph away. Detective Daniels sees Eileen Morgan and her cameraman.

Detective Daniels walks over to Eileen Morgan, "Can I say something?"

Eileen nods, "Of course."

Eileen motions to her cameraman.

The camera comes on and Eileen introduces Detective Daniels, "Hi, this is Eileen Morgan. I'm outside the courthouse as the trial of Joseph Thompson ends for the day. I'm with Detective Pamela Daniels, one of the detectives responsible for apprehending Joseph Thompson." Eileen turns to Detective Daniels, "Detective, do you have anything you would like to say?"

Detective Daniels looks at the camera, "I just want everyone to know that what I said in court today was because of my job. Now, I must speak with what is in my heart." She pauses, "Joseph Thompson saved my life. He helped make this a better city, a safer city. I am eternally grateful for that. I admire his strength of character and the fact that he did all of this for love. If we only had more people out there willing to stand up for what is right, we may be able to start healing this world. I truly wish he was still out there. Thank you."

No one could believe what Detective Daniels said. On his hour out of isolation that night, Joseph watches the interview with Detective Daniels. He smiles to himself as he realizes that he even reached Detective Daniels with what he had done.

DATE - September 10th, 2000
San Francisco, CA

Joseph sits in his cell late at night. He has been thinking about his two years as the Silent Knight and how he got to this point in his life.

Joseph hears Kristen's voice, "I'm so proud of you Joseph."

Joseph looks over and sees Kristen, "The Silent Knight is over. I made things right."

The jailor looks at his monitor. He sees Joseph talking and wonders who Joseph is talking to.

Kristen smiles, "Yes you did, but the story of the Silent Knight will live forever."

Joseph gets a little choked up, "I miss you so much."

Kristen moves a little closer, "Things are right on Earth again, but not in our hearts."

Joseph nods slowly, "It's time for us to be together again. The world doesn't need me anymore."

Kristen smiles, "You know what you must do now." She pauses, "And now you also know why you were put on this Earth and what was so special and unique about you."

As Kristen's image disappears, Joseph remembers the last time he heard those words. The village elder knew all those years ago. Joseph contemplates his next move. He knows what he must do. It's time to move on and be with Kristen again.

DATE - October 6th, 2000
San Francisco, CA

The courtroom is packed full of citizens, reporters and law enforcement. Mr. Reid stands up and prepares to start his defense. He looks around the courtroom and then to the jury.

Mr. Reid speaks with a powerful voice, "Everyone here knows that crime has dropped in San Francisco thanks to Joseph Thompson, but did you know that the number of violent crimes have dropped all over the country. He didn't just make our city safer, he made the country a safer place." He pauses, "The United States is the greatest country in the world, but we do have our share of problems. We rely on law enforcement and our judicial system to remove those problems, but what happens when the system fails, like it did for Joseph Thompson when his future wife was murdered right in front of him and the man that did it was not punished. He took a stand. He made sure it wouldn't happen to one of us. Surely ladies and gentlemen, you can see what drove Joseph Thompson to do what he did." He pauses, then continues in a more loving tone, "If not, let me explain. It was love, the love for Kristen Shobe and the rest of us. Thank you."

The defense lawyer calls his first witness, Mr. Lee. As Mr. Lee takes the stand, Mr. Dawson sits back in his chair, knowing that the opening statement alone won the case for the defense. He wonders how he could possibly get a conviction now.

DATE - November 15th, 2000
San Francisco, CA

The last of the reporters file into the courtroom as the judge bangs his gavel, "Order, everyone quiet down. Court is now in session."

The judge looks over to Mr. Reid, "I understand that the defendant wants to make a statement."

Mr. Reid stands, "That is correct your honor."

The judge looks at Mr. Dawson and Mr. Dawson replies, "No objection your honor."

Mr. Reid looks over at Joseph, "Are you sure about this?"

Joseph nods and stands up, "First, I would like to say that I am the Silent Knight. Second, I did kill 279 known criminals over the two years I was on the streets."

Mr. Dawson is completely taken off guard by what he just heard. A collective gasp comes over the courtroom.

The defense lawyer lets out a sigh and the judge speaks, "Mr. Thompson, are you aware of your rights about self-incrimination?"

Joseph nods knowingly, "I'm completely aware of all my constitutional rights your honor. Mr. Reid explained them all to me."

The judge nods, "Okay, then continue."

Joseph takes a breath, "I was perfectly sane when I did this. I knew exactly what I was doing. I know I affected everyone here, even you your honor. What scares me the most is that a jury would find me not guilty. I don't believe you can find twelve citizens anywhere in this country that would convict me for what I did." Joseph pauses, "This world has a long way to go, but I believe it can get there. I believe we all can live free and equal, not worrying about all the violence and prejudice. It all starts with love, love is a powerful thing. Love can change the world." Joseph pauses once more, "So I end with this, I am changing my plea to guilty."

Another collective gasp comes over the courtroom as no one can believe what they just heard and people start whispering to each other.

The judge bangs his gavel, "Order, everyone quiet down." He looks at Joseph, "Is there anything else Mr. Thompson?"

Joseph continues, "Yes your honor. I would like to request the death penalty and if I get the death penalty, I would like it to occur on February 14th." He sighs, "It's time for me to be with Kristen again. The world doesn't need me anymore." He pauses, "That's all your honor."

Mr. Dawson is still in shock, not able to even comprehend any kind of an objection.

The judge picks up his gavel, "It appears that I have a lot to consider and Mr. Reid and Mr. Dawson has a lot to talk about." He bangs down his gavel, "This court is adjourned for the day."

DATE - December 21st, 2000
San Francisco, CA

First thing in the morning, Mr. Reid and Mr. Dawson walk into the judge's chamber. The three of them sit down to discuss what went on in court.

The judge speaks, "Mr. Reid, have you had a chance to talk with your client?"

Mr. Reid nods, "Yes I have your honor."

The judge replies, "And has your client changed his mind?"

Mr. Reid shakes his head, "No your honor. I've tried to talk to him about other possible actions, but he won't even consider anything else."

The judge questions the defense lawyer, "Do you think he will take his own life if we deny his request?"

Mr. Reid nods completely sure of himself, "I believe so."

Mr. Dawson finally speaks up, "He is guilty. No one wants to be the bad guy in all of this, but what he did warrants the death penalty." He pauses, "Everyone went into this trial not wanting to be the person responsible for sending the Silent Knight away, but Mr. Thompson has removed that factor from the equation."

The judge nods, "I see your point, and it's a good one. The defendant is in control and it appears he is wanting this. The psychological evaluation Mr. Thompson took at the beginning of the trial shows that he is depressed, but still mentally capable of making a rational decision." He pauses, "Has the family tried to make a motion to quash Mr. Thompson's request?"

Mr. Reid shakes his head, "No your honor. In fact, when I spoke to them, they fully support his decision."

The judge nods slightly, "This is the biggest decision of my career." He pauses for a second, "I'm going to allow the requests of the death penalty and when it is to happen."

Mr. Reid speaks, "In that case your honor, Mr. Thompson has one more thing he would like to request."

Mr. Dawson responds, "What's that?"

Mr. Reid explains, "He wants to visit Kristen Shobe's grave with Detective Daniels and Detective Jackson the morning of February 14th and he wants to be able to take a candle and matches with him."

The judge looks at the DA, "How do you feel about the visit to the grave?"

Mr. Dawson sighs, "I'm not sure we should allow it your honor. He might have some hidden reason for wanting to go there."

Mr. Reid speaks up, "I don't see a problem at all. He turned himself in and he hasn't given any problems since he was taken into custody. Plus, we are going to have two detectives present."

The judge sits back, "I would have to agree with Mr. Reid, but we will have to talk about it at a later time. The trial will resume on Monday and I will announce my decision on the request."

The lawyers nod in agreement and leave the judge's chambers.

DATE - January 17th, 2001
San Francisco, CA

That night, Joseph is sitting on his bed in his cell. Joseph hears movement outside his cell and he looks over to the cell door. Joseph lets out a slight smile as Detective Daniels and Detective Jackson enter his cell. Detective Daniels sits next to him on the bunk and Detective Jackson stands across from them.

Joseph questions, "Anything new?"

Detective Daniels nods, "The new headstone is already in place."

Detective Jackson speaks up, "The visit was hard to get, but the DA finally agreed to it."

Joseph smiles, "Good, now all I have to do is wait."

Detective Daniels shakes her head, "I don't understand all of this."

Joseph looks at her, "Have you ever felt love so strong
you couldn't live without it? Have you ever met your one,
true love?"

Detective Daniels sighs, "No."

Joseph smiles at her, "When you do, then you'll understand everything."

Detective Jackson speaks up, "We better go. We just
wanted to stop in and let you know what is going on."

Joseph nods, "Thank you, for everything."

The two detectives leave and Joseph drifts off to sleep.
He dreams of Kristen. His mind replays their entire lives
together and he watches as if it were a movie. From the
time they first met as kids, to falling in love at their senior
prom. The first time they made love, the beach, the fishing,
the trip to Mexico and getting engaged rush through his
mind. This time the story doesn't end with Kristen's death,
but with the two of them standing at a heavenly alter,
dressed for a wedding.

Epilogue

DATE - February 14th, 2001
San Francisco, CA

It's 7 am on a cool, overcast morning as a car pulls into the Parkview Cemetery. Detective Jackson parks the car about a quarter mile into the cemetery. Detective Jackson, Detective Daniels and Joseph get out of the car. The three of them walk about twenty five yards from the car, over near a large oak tree, and they arrive at Kristen's grave. The three of them look down at the new, gray marble headstone that lays flat against the ground. It is an extended headstone that contains two names.

Centered at the top of the headstone is carved the words, "Eternal Love". Just below those words, on the left hand side from looking down at the headstone from in front of it is carved the name, "Kristen L. Shobe". Just below the name is carved the words, "Born: Feb 14th, 1973". Just below that date is carved the words, "Died: Sep 28th, 1997".

Just below the words eternal love, on the right hand side from looking down at the headstone from in front of it, is carved the name, "Joseph W. Thompson". Just below that name is carved the words, "Born: Jan 1st, 1973". Just below that date is carved the words, "Died: Feb 14th, 2001". Centered at the bottom of the headstone is a small carved out circle.

Joseph kneels down and places a candle in the carved out circle at the bottom. He lights the candle and stands back up.

Joseph speaks as tears come to his eyes, "Kristen was such a beautiful person. Her love knew no bounds. I loved her more than life itself. My life ended when she was murdered. All I had left were the memories and this candle."

The two detectives are not sure what Joseph is trying to say and Joseph continues, "Our love ends if this candle ever stops burning. It's an eternal flame for an eternal love." Joseph pauses, then looks at Detective Daniels, "I have a favor to ask you."

Detective Daniels gets a puzzled look, "What is it?"

Joseph sighs, "Promise me, as I promised Kristen when she died in my arms, that you will come here every year on this day and light a candle as I have. To keep the eternal flame burning."

Detective Daniels chuckles nervously, "But why me?"

Joseph smiles, "I know I can trust you, I just feel it. Besides, I just have a feeling Kristen would want it to be you."

Detective Daniels looks at the headstone and the burning candle. Her heart beats a little faster, but she is unsure why. She wonders what Kristen was like.

Detective Daniels takes Joseph's hand not knowing exactly why she is saying the words that come out, "I promise Joseph. I'll do it."

The three of them turn and walk away. At 11 pm that night, Joseph would be by Kristen's side at that heavenly alter. Now they are together forever, and the eternal flame continues to burn.

The End